# STORMS CORP

# STORMS CORP

## THE AMBER DOCUMENTS

### ANSUNET STRYDOM

authorHOUSE®

*AuthorHouse™*
*1663 Liberty Drive*
*Bloomington, IN 47403*
*www.authorhouse.com*
*Phone: 1-800-839-8640*

*The author made use of real place names but all characters and events are fictional.*

*Published by AuthorHouse    08/09/2012*

*ISBN:978-1-4772-2244-7 (sc)*
*ISBN: 978-1-4772-2243-0 (e)*

# CHAPTER 1

# THE CONVERSATION

Elizabeth and her parents had a suburban home in London, but her father decided to move to Johannesburg, South Africa, where he thought Elizabeth would be save from dangerous terrorist attacks that recently targeted London.

It was an exciting Saturday morning for Elizabeth Storms, for her 16ᵗʰ birthday is on Monday. Elizabeth a beautiful fifteen year old, blue eyed brunette, and going on sixteen Monday, her father Jeff Storms, with dark brown hair and brown eyes, decided to give Elizabeth a birthday bash two days before her birthday. Elizabeth invited Milan over to help her with the decorations.

'Where's Milan, she was suppose to be here by now.' she grunted as she paced in front of the door. She saw a black Mercedes pull up in front of their mansion through the living room window.

'Uh, here she is now' she said to herself. Milan got out of the car, and started to walk towards the front door. Elizabeth opened the door silently, and saw the back of Milan waving goodbye to her mother.

'Hey, Milan!' she shouted.

Milan screamed in a high pitched voice while turning around, and started to laugh, Milan was a Chinese girl with long black hair, and maroon red highlights and she had very stylish reading glasses on, and is the smartest in the class.

'Nice highlights.' Elizabeth complemented her, making a fake smile.

'Thanks, I just had them done.' Milan said brushing herself up.

'Cool.' Elizabeth said as she opened the door wider for Milan to enter.

The entrance to the Storms house was magnificent, a spiral staircase on the left with sandstone bricks. The uneven cut makes it fit in with the entrance. Elizabeth and Milan walk away from the entrance and headed for the living room. The couches were royal blue, and the smell of Jasmine made you feel like you were in a field full of them. On one of the royal blue velvet couches stood three boxes.

'What shall we start with?' Elizabeth asked pointing to the three boxes with decorations inside it. William Storms a handsome brunette, blue eyed had entered the room. Milan had gotten nervous when he did, she was secretly crushing on William and Elizabeth knew all about it.

'Hi William.' she sighed happily.

'Hi, I think you should start with this.' he said and took pink organza out of the box and waving it around, like a ribbon dancer.

'Thank you, William' she said as she gritted her teeth.

'Pleasure my dear, ooh! I'm Elizabeth, and today is my birthday, LA, LA, LA. Happy birthday little sis' he hugged her and gave her a kiss on the forehead.

'Awww' Milan sighed again looking at Elizabeth who cleared her throat, and spoke again.

'He's right, we should start with that.' Milan said as William put the pink organza back in the box.

Milan took the pink organza, and hung a piece by the front door.

Elizabeth hung "HAPPY BIRTHDAY" in the dining room.

# 1 HOUR LATER

## ARRIVALS

The rest of Elizabeth's friends have arrived one by one. Daniel was the first to arrive, he had light brown hair, and dark brown eyes, and he has a little crush on Elizabeth. Shortly after Daniel's arrival, Melissa arrived. She had red hair and green eyes. The next to arrive was Mia, a Spanish girl with black hair, and brown eyes. The next to arrive was Miguel; he has brown hair, and blue eyes. Clayton arrives five minutes later; he has light brown hair, and has blue grey eyes. The last to arrive was James he's older than the rest. He has dark brown hair, and brown eyes. After the long line of arrivals of friends, Elizabeth and Milan were both exhausted hosting.

Elizabeth's mother is always busy working and handling cases overseas, her father said she's an extremely good manager at the Corporation, so she couldn't make it to Elizabeth's birthday bash. Jeff Storms a mid-aged man with grey hairs in between those brunettes, and light blue eyes, Elizabeth's father, just got off the phone with her mother, "Lizzie Storms a mid-aged woman with beautiful golden brown hair and blue eyes."

'Err, Elizabeth . . . there's a live satellite message for you on your computer.' he mentioned to Elizabeth who was laughing with her friends and eating cake. She dropped the fork and napkin on the table, and started to run out the dining room. She ran across the entrance and to the spiral staircase and raced towards her room, and closed the door behind her. Her mother meant everything to her; she looked up to her mother. The sound of alternative rock music playing in the background calmed her down a little. She took a deep breath, and sat down in front of her computer then logged on to find a video message waiting for her, she turned the little camera, on top of her computer on. Elizabeth looks like a younger version of her mother.

'Hi, Elizabeth how's the birthday bash.' she asked smiling at Elizabeth. Her brown hair hanging down her shoulders rather roughly.

'It's going great mommy . . . where are you?' she asked listening to the traffic in the background.

'I'm in New York, official business for the corporation, I'll be back before Monday, I'm leaving tonight, OK.' she replied

'You better . . . I miss you, dad misses you even William misses' you.' she said sadly looking down into her lap, and looking up again.

'I'm sorry, I have to miss your birthday bash it won't happen again.' she replied with guilt.

'It's OK mom, it only happens once a year anyway.' she said knowingly that her mother is feeling guilty for not be there for her birthday bash.

'You'll get your present after your day's work at the corporation . . .' she faked laughed and then silently looking at Elizabeth's face expression, she looked surprised.

Elizabeth got up from her chair and started pacing up and down.

'I hope you are not mad.' her eyes following Elizabeth's pacing.

'Mad, this is great, I have a job I'll take the employment.' she agreed with a frown. 'Bye mom.'

'Bye honey, see you Monday.' she replied and logged off.

Elizabeth got up from the chair and looked around her room; her mother would say it's a picture gallery. Her room was full of posters. Just one picture of Danny Redburn a British actor, cute and blue dreamy eyes and dark hair, above her bed next to a picture she drew from a photo of herself smiling, then she walked over to her dressing table and looked in the mirror and smiled. Elizabeth walked towards the door, and opened it. Before she left, she looked at Danny Redburn's poster and smiled and shut the door. Elizabeth went downstairs to the TV room where she suspected all her friends would be sitting. As she approached the TV room, she heard laughing as it would seem they were watching something funny. The curtains were drawn closed and heads turned when Elizabeth entered the room. Milan was the first to stand up and talk to Elizabeth.

'So, what did your mother say?' Milan asked breathlessly.

'Milan, she told me that I just became an employee at Storms Corporation. Why?' she asked looking at her father, then her friends.

'We're sorry Elizabeth it was suppose to be a surprise. When you were younger you always said you wanted to be part of the corporation. I can only employ you now that you are sixteen.' her father explained. 'You know I could use a PA' her father said walking to her and hugging her.

'Thanks Dad.' Elizabeth said hugging her father tightly.

'Come on lets go play a good game of challenging tennis.' her father ordered happily.

'Go I'll be there in a sec, I'm just going to fetch the tennis rackets in the storage room.' Elizabeth said. Daniel looked at Elizabeth leave them and head for the passageway under the stairs. He looked at Clayton who signalled him to go for it.

'I'll help you.' Daniel offered, and followed Elizabeth.

Daniel and Elizabeth walked off to the passage Daniel had never been to this part of the house before. The passage was rather wide with Persian matting of excellent wine red colour on the floor. Portraits and paintings of the Storm's ancestors were hanging on each side of the wall as they passed. When they finally reached the storage room, Daniel looked at the wardrobe with a mirror on the door next to the door to the storage room. He looked at himself and he felt as though nothing could get in his way to ask Elizabeth out. Daniel had entered the storage room after Elizabeth, but she had her back to him. A few seconds later Daniel and Elizabeth heard a mouse squeak. Elizabeth slowly looked down her eyes widened and then she screamed loud and event louder.

'Help me Daniel!' she shouted.

Daniel laughed and picked the mouse up by its tail, his wide smile made Elizabeth flinch.

'Mm . . . Do you think your father will allow me to keep this mouse?' Daniel laughed.

'Well you can have him . . . urgh!' Elizabeth said disgusted.

The house keeper came to stand at the door, more alert than he was before looking alarmed at Daniel and the mouse in his hand.

'Is everything alright here? Mamouselle Elizabeth.' he asked looking at Daniel again. Pierre looked back at Elizabeth as he spoke with his French accent, rather old looking but he is a loyal house keeper to the Storms family.

'Yes, Pierre Daniel has . . . well . . . it.' she said pointing at the mouse in Daniel's hand, and putting a brown lock of hair behind her ear.

Pierre looked into Daniel's hand, and smiled faintly, then walked away. Elizabeth looked at Daniel.

'Thank you . . .' she paused as she looked at Daniel and at the mouse, she quivered. 'We better get going, and get rid of that thing.' she said, imagining the look on her face when she got scared, and started to laugh at herself.

Daniel set the mouse free outside the small window, and then helped Elizabeth with the tennis rackets, and balls.

When they got to the front door, Daniel put the bag of tennis
balls down on the floor and opened the door.

'OK I admit it that was a bit funny.' Elizabeth laughed clutching
the tennis balls, as the bag nearly fell. Daniel smiled as he attempted
to help her.

Daniel wanted to cough up the courage to tell her something.
Pierre had come from the kitchen side smirking at them as he
passed to go upstairs.

Daniel placed the bag of tennis rackets on the floor, and opened
the door for her, looking at her intently to catch a glimpse of her
beautiful eyes.

'Thanks.' she replied looking at Daniel her eyes lit up when she
smiled.

'You know, I'd do anything for you.' Daniel said in admiration
and he smiled and bowed, letting her go passed him. They walked
around the house when they finally reached a small gravel pathway
heading out to the tennis courts. A tennis ball had fallen out of
the bag, on Elizabeth's foot.

'Oh, damn mouse. Eats everything.' she said angrily as she and
Daniel attempted to pick it up at the same time. They bumped
heads, and fell to the ground.

'Sorry.' Daniel apologized and helps Elizabeth to her feet. He
bent over alone and picked up the ball, and they smiled at each

other and Daniel's stomach dropped. They turned to head for the tennis courts.

'Uh . . . finally we were just about to send out a search party.' Elizabeth's father joked.

Elizabeth looked at Daniel strangely and then walked to her father, while Miguel, Clayton and James ran towards Daniel.

'Dad have you ever thought of putting, rattex in the storage. I embarrassed myself in front of Daniel.' she squirmed, squeezing a tennis ball that finally popped out of her hand and hit her father's chin.

'Oh . . . ow!' he stepped back holding his chin. 'Sorry Dad.' she apologized and approached him

Daniel, Clayton Miguel and James look over at Elizabeth and her father as she tends to aid him. Clayton then shrugged Daniels sleeve.

'Did you ask her?' Clayton asked. 'The Dance is a week away.' he stated, trying not to laugh at Daniel's face.

'No, there was a damn field mouse.' Daniel grunted.

'Come on guys let's start with the game.' Elizabeth's father ordered as Elizabeth stepped away from her father and ran to her side of the court. Daniel walked rather slowly and looking down at his tennis racket.

'Come on Dan, let's get to it today!' Elizabeth shouted from across the court. Daniel laughed and turned around to face her and she already served but it hit the net.

'Dang it!' she cursed as Clayton ran to fetch the ball to throw it back at her. 'I was hoping to surprise you.' she smiled naughtily.

She tried again, the ball was on its way down as she jumped to hit it and the ball flew over the net straight to Daniel. Daniel had to run to hit the ball back to Elizabeth he nearly missed it. Elizabeth hits the ball back to Daniel with full force, but he missed it.

'Wow that was a strong ball Elizabeth.' Daniel honoured her strong hit that nearly hit him in the chest if he didn't move.

'Thanks Dan, but maybe you can give me a stronger game next time.' She said while Milan, Melissa and Mia were cheering her on and the boys where silent as they thought cheering for Daniel wouldn't help at all.

Elizabeth is the captain of the tennis team at school, and proves how good she is in this game with Daniel. She is the best player in the team, hence the title "Captain".

## SATURDAY NIGHT

After an excellent party and everyone left, Milan was the only one remaining. They came hopping down the stairs and singing in perfect harmony, they finally reached the stairs and stopped singing when William came into the room.

'Oh, thank goodness you stopped singing . . . urge terrible.' William joked and walked out the front door, as Milan laughed out loud.

'Come on I want to show you something.' Elizabeth grabbed Milan's hands as friends do, and pulled her into the direction she wanted to go. They leapt through the kitchen passed Mr. Storms and out the back door. 'Uh . . . Elizabeth . . .' Mr Storms shouted from the kitchen, she stopped and came back to the door.

'Yes, father?' she asked assertively.

Milan's mother will be here any sec. Where are you going anyway?' Mr. Storms asked, taking his glasses of his face, and tilt his head forward, as though Elizabeth and Milan were five.

'Daddy, I want to show Milan the . . .' she was interrupted by the doorbell and sighed rather big. ' . . . swimming pool, her voice dies away as they re-enter the house.

They walk through the kitchen.

'I will see it on Monday, Elizabeth.' Milan smiled

'I want to give you a plan, of what I wanted us to do once the pool is finished.' she sighed. 'But alright, Monday it is.' she smiled as they were now approaching the front door where Milan's mother stood and waited patiently.

'Hi Mrs. Cho' Elizabeth said with a smile, and gave her a hug like she was her own mother. Elizabeth has just said goodbye to Milan. She waved goodbye to Milan and her mother, and closed the door.

'Hey great game out there, today . . . so there is already an office for you at work, all you need to do is show yourself, oh, and it's on the top floor.' he sat down and explained, as Elizabeth entered the kitchen.

'Dad this isn't one of your briefings, talk to me like I am your daughter please.' Elizabeth said firmly, as she leaned forward to lay her head down.

'OK, I will . . . I just thought I would tell you where your desk is, sorry it came out brief-mode.' he apologised with a snigger.

'Where was William headed anyway? Daddy . . .' she paused as he seemed to get lost in the newspaper again.

'He is umm . . . um, he left to get some work done at the company.' he said as he wasn't sure himself. Elizabeth rolled her eyes as if impatient.

## LATER

Elizabeth opened her eyes rather slowly with that urge just to sit up and bare the rumble in her stomach. She had loads of things on her mind, it was late, dark and everyone else was sleeping.

She headed for the stairs down the passage in her silver silk with black stars pyjamas; she stepped quietly down the stairs into the kitchen.

Elizabeth just started to make her midnight snack, as she knew this was not her imagination she heard voices that seemed to be in the storage room. She looked down the passage way from the kitchen. She silently places the butter knife on the counter and slightly tip-toeing down the passage way to the storage room. The antique chest was standing on the side of the passage with a little purple vase on it, no one seemed to see this side of the house at times, and the purple vase has been there for years. Elizabeth's gown must have swerve into it and knock it over, she heard it roll as it came to the edge it fell and broke into a million pieces. She had to think fast as it seemed the people in the storage heard the crashing of the vase. She then ran to the wardrobe on the other side of the passage and hid behind it.

'Hello?' she heard an unrecognized voice come from the storage room, as she held her breath.

'Jeff, I swear you have ghosts.' the one man laughed, after the pause. Elizabeth later heard the door close and the voices sounded shallower.

A little bewildered and tired Elizabeth heads back to the kitchen. She finishes her midnight snack cleans up, as she headed for her room she peered down to the kitchen door, she left the light on. She quickly ran down, and just after she switched the kitchen light off, the store door had opened and her father and the other two men came down the passage. Elizabeth ran into the TV room next to the kitchen. What she overheard was this:

*'He sets out a great danger to my daughter; I want him in and out before she gets there, tomorrow.'*

*'Of course, sir.' the one man said*

*'. . . and Tshepo . . .'* Jeff said as they walked on

*'I want you and your son to be on parameter in and around Storms Corp. tomorrow too. I want you to notify me when she comes. Vince is no one's picnic.'*

'Vince?!?' she whispered.

*'I will do that, thanks for having me in your humble home.'*

*'Anytime, you are welcome anytime Tshepo.'* Elizabeth heard her father say assertively; few minutes thereafter she heard the door close.

She peered out of the TV room door and saw her father retreat to his Library, this was her chance to sneak up to her room and get some rest

# CHAPTER 2

## IT'S IN HER BLOOD

Monday morning and Elizabeth was excited and warmed up at the same time. She is excited that she will start her first day of work after school. At the multi-millionaire spy company, that's taking down some of the worlds most dangerous criminals. Elizabeth went to her bathroom to take a shower.

'Elizabeth! Phone call.' her father said through the door.

'OK, Dad, I'll get it here.' she said to her father, still clutching her towel tightly around her and hoping her father does not enter.

'OK, breakfast is almost ready.' he replied. She put the phone against her ear.

'Come on this better be quick, I'm getting cold.' she thought.

'Hello . . . who am I speaking to?'

'Ah, yes this is TL, from Harrismith. Miss Storms your wonderful idea is complete.' Emma joked.

'That's great when do I get them?' Elizabeth asked without hesitation.

'Well, whenever you want.' Emma replied

'I want them in the spring.' She said excitedly, jumping up and down.

'OK, see you then . . . bye. May I also speak to William?' Emma replied laughing nervously.

'Bye Emma . . .'WILL, PHONE!' Elizabeth shouted excitedly and waits for her brother to answer before she put down the phone.

Elizabeth ran to her chest of drawers, and took out her school socks and underclothes; she took out her school clothes from her wardrobe, threw it on her bed and started to dress as quickly as possible. Well it was nearly the end of winter but it is still cold. Elizabeth went downstairs to eat breakfast at the hand crafted table that her ancestors had made. She found her mother there, sipping a cup of coffee.

'Hello, mom . . . when did you get back?' Elizabeth asked happily.

'Very late last night. When I came in, I saw your father's office door open, and there he was inside, waiting for me.' she said with a wide smile.

'It's obviously about that meeting.' she whispered softly while taking a sip of orange juice, hoping that no one would hear her.

William walked in at the same moment, all dressed and ready to go, wearing a suit, while it's actually casual day at the company.

'Uh, Will it's casual day today" Jeff said keeping his laugh in.

'Did you forget, or did that phone call make you forget.' Elizabeth joked.

Elizabeth tried not to laugh, as she found this very hilarious, but had held her laugh eventually. Her brother came to sit right opposite her, and eating like a pig. Elizabeth started to munch her corn flakes irritably.

'OK . . . stop it you two, Elizabeth your brother is just joking.' her mother said firmly.

There is a car hooting outside. Elizabeth ran to the front door picked up her back pack, ran out the door. It was Milan and her mother, waiting in the new Audi TTi for her. Elizabeth's family saw the car went out of the grounds. The three of them gathered around the handcrafted table, to discuss what had happened last night in the storage room.

'OK, I've got it handled, my best co-workers, were here on Saturday night, and they bringing him in today.' he said and took a sip of coffee.

'That's great, when?' his wife asked suddenly

'Oh, probably around two o'clock.' he replied, taking Elizabeth's bowl and putting it in the sink.

Lizzie looked at her watch.

'Oh! I have to go to work.' she said as she rushed out of the house without saying goodbye.

'William, I want you to do something for me today? Jeff asked his son.

'Yes father anytime.' William replied with curiosity.

'What I want you to do is, retrieve a microchip for me. It will be about the size of a car when you look out of my office window from the top floor. OK. Can you do it?' he asked.

'Of course, this will be easy, won't it? I mean I've done much more dangerous tasks than this' William smiled 'Uncle Tomas gives me all the easy tasks.'

'Remember he's still your uncle.'

'Yeah, but he's no good. He sucks at this job, please dad can't you fire him? He'll become part of the 'Fire Brigade' we've put together.' he begged while he laughed.

'First I can't fire him, because he's an asset to this company. Sorry it's just funny when you said "Fire Brigade". I mean where you came up with that?' he laughed.

'A friend told me about it. Besides he only handles the debt . . ."

'Exactly, he's good at it. When we were teenagers in University, he did my accounting for me. And back then we were still in London at Oxford too! Trust me he was a nerd.' he laughed.

'Oh . . . that's why I can't stand him, he's a nerd. Great.' William grunted.

'Don't be upset, he's just not yet part of the "Fire Brigade" William. That word is just hilarious for the people that we fired.' he laughed, while he put his coffee cup in the sink.

'Well, you two are twins. I thought you'd be the same.' William said frowning. William hand his cup to his father to put in the sink.

'We are I was just lazy back then. I didn't know the basics of accounting. Should we go? We're going to be late.' he said seriously.

'Sure, uh where is this microchip?' he asked.

'It's somewhere in New York. If you have noticed, your mother was in New York, but found nothing.' he said taking his briefcase from the chair, walking to the front door with William.

'OK, when do I leave?' he asked.

'Tonight . . . The jet leaves at eight.' He said plainly.

'Really tonight?' he asked excitedly.

'Yes, and I expect you in my office Friday afternoon.' he said closing the front door behind them, and heading for the Mercedes convertible in the drive way.

William and his father leave the home and wave goodbye to the guards who stood in front of the gates.

'Yes . . . But if Elizabeth is going to ask questions.'

'Like what the microchip is?' he paused looking at his father's expression.

'You don't think she knows do you?' his father asked.

'No. What isn't she suppose to know?' William asked, looking away from his father, and putting his attention to the road.

'Well she was acting a bit weird this morning.' he said to himself.

'What are you talking about?' William asked confused.

'Yeah, that's not it. Now I remember I saw a palm of her hand on the mirror of the wardrobe. She was there, so she does know about Vincent. Coming to my office at two this afternoon.' he said and started to accelerate.

'Elizabeth's school only comes out at two, and by the time she gets to the company we'll be finished with the meeting.'

'Yeah, but she's capable of anything, like your mother and you.' He finished with a smile.

'What do you mean?' William asked frowning with great amusement.

'When you were ten or eleven you always got your way, no matter what the consequences. There was that one time when you were thirteen, you wanted tickets to a concert, but you were underage and you had to take us with you. So your mother and I kept it a secret, and tried to make you forget about the concert. You found out about this secret that we were not going to take you to the concert. You took it quite well, then a few hours later you came back, and said you got the three remaining tickets for the concert, you even got it right to get the last remaining VIP tickets, but you gave them to your friends. To let them feel the glory for once.' he laughed.

'Really, which concert? Was it at school?' he asked.

'No! It was a rock concert, "Giant Antz". Do you remember them?' He asked as he slowed down to pull in at the private parking lot.

'Nope, it doesn't ring a bell "Giant Antz" . . . no I really can't remember them, was it a band or a solo singer?' he asked as his father heading for the back entrance.

'It was a band.' he replied with enthusiasm, Jeff stopped the convertible and they both got out of the car as Matthew approached them. Jeff gave the car keys to Matthew, the Storms Corporation Valet.

'Thanks Matthew.' Jeff smiled

'No problem Mr. Storms'

'So what did Emma say, did she say she's coming, if so we can always prepare the table for one more.' William stopped and looked at his father, then finally spoke.

'She said she's coming but she won't be staying with us, she'll be staying with her aunt, because she wants to leave the following morning early. She told me there's someone following her around, Emma wouldn't tell me who, I bet you, it's Danny, he's probably trying to find information about her headquarters, and she doesn't want to stay away that long.' he said smartly as Tomas came bursting out the back door yelling.

'JEFF, JEFF, WE HAVE A PROBLEM, SOMETHING'S WRONG WITH ANNA . . ."

'What! Tell me what happened.' he asked worried.

'I don't know . . .' William rolled his eyes; Tomas spotted him then carried on speaking. 'She came back badly injured, with bruises and cuts as if she's been held hostage by some one.' Tomas cried.

'Wills . . . we have a situation here.' Jeff turned to his son and then turned to Tomas. 'Did she say anything about the people that hurt her?' Jeff asked anxiously

'No, all I heard was "The Other Side" then she passed out and we took her to the hospital, where she is right now.' Tomas explained, as Anna comes from behind Tomas and Jeff, but William noticed her and realized it was a practical joke, he starts to speak, trying to stop himself from laughing and played along.

'And you couldn't phone to tell us this? Dad, it's a bad ass gang, they're called "The Other Side" and Tomas assigned the task to Anna. Not too long ago they stole a gigantic diamond from the biggest museum in Amsterdam. Anna is just a two year junior agent and you sent her there.' he acted, Anna had started to laugh silently.

With all the commotion one of the office secretaries came out followed by other junior agents.

'I didn't mean to, I thought she'd be able to handle it.'

'Tomas your job is to handle company assets, not begin a drama club.' William said sly.

'What?'

Unfortunately the Oscar® must go to me, because Anna is standing right behind both of you, and she looks angry.' William finally burst out laughing, Tomas and Jeff turned around sheepishly.

'Sorry, it didn't work guys, but maybe next time you'll think twice before playing a trick on me, remember I'm a S.C.A Agent and solving cases is my speciality.' William said, and then Anna started to yell.

'Tomas Andrew Storms, I said no! And besides I told William about all my missions, he would know what you were talking about.'

'So, how was this one Anna?' William asked confidently.

'Fine, how was your ride with "Mr. Scamming" here. By the way, congratulations William, it's your fifth anniversary of being an agent here at Storms Corp.' Anna said angrily looking at Jeff.

'Oh yes, Tomas we have to reschedule an appointment at two.' Jeff said with a smile on his face.

'Dad, Elizabeth's not interested in Vince anymore and the way that he hurt her I just feel like beating him up.' William said angrily.

'OK, just as you say Wills, now can we please go inside, I feel kind of awkward.' Jeff said to the three of them, as William giggled softly.

'Dad, it is a good idea if Elizabeth comes earlier than expected, she must get a feel of what Storms Corporation is all about.' William said, as they got into the elevator with Tomas and Anna.

'Elizabeth is coming today, why wasn't I told about this?' Tomas asked and then looked at William.

'You wanna know why we didn't tell you that she's coming today.' he said, and Tomas nodded.

'OK, so um the reason why we didn't tell you was that you're an asset to this company, and you're the one that is not suppose to know everything about what's going on in Storms Corp., you get the picture?' William explained wisely.

'Yeah, uh, I totally get the picture.' Tomas smiled. As the computerized elevator announced the floor that he must get off.

'Anna, are you coming?' he asked.

'Err, no I'm up one level. Thanks though.' Anna said with a wide smile. The elevator doors closed with Tomas turning around and walking away. Anna started to lecture William.

'You should not have been so hard on him.' Anna said looking at William angrily.

'Oh, yeah why didn't you go with him? That's your floor Anna.' William said as he crossed his arms and raised his eyebrows.

'I don't comfort people Will, I attack them, I'm an SCA agent, and you know what, we're just as good as the "CIA®". The only difference is they solve crimes and go straight after the bad guy, and we retrieve stolen goods to their owners, it's a shame they don't make a "Hit TV Series" about us.' she replied with a wishful smile.

'Oh, my . . . gosh, you're jealous. Dad I don't believe this, she's jealous of the "CIA®" and we're just as good as them.' he laughed with the awareness that the subject has changed. The computerized elevator then announced the 70th floor.

'Well, it looks like I'm gonna have to walk down twenty steps.' she smiled and left as the doors started to close. William and his father looked at each other, and they started to laugh.

'You're going to transfer her, right.' William said now holding in his laugh.

'Not in an accidental moment, I mean in her dreams.' Jeff stopped laughing when finally they reached the top floor, and once again the computerized elevator, announced the 230TH floor. They walked out of the elevator, silent and without any expression.

'Tell me when you're going to leave' he said and walked towards his glass office.

'Sure' William said, and walked to the other side of the building silently smiling.

# AT ELIZABETH'S SCHOOL

The bell rang for lunch break, Elizabeth and her friends went out to lunch at a restaurant nearby. Elizabeth sat down first and started to speak, while the others were getting into their original seats that they sat in everyday during break. The waitress came up to them.

'What will you be eating today Miss Storms?' the waitress asked happily.

'The usual, remember the hamburger the tomato and onion . . .''

'Must be at the top, I know.' the waitress laughed.

'And the tomato sauce must be at the bottom of the patty and a salad this time, please.' Elizabeth continued.

'OK, the rest of you, you'll . . .''

'Take the usual.' they all said at once and laughed.

The waitress walked away to place their order at the kitchen. Elizabeth leaned forward as soon as the waitress was out of sight.

'OK, I eavesdropped on my father last night; I was on my way to the kitchen for a midnight snack, when I heard voices in the storage room, where Daniel and I were getting the tennis rackets.' at that moment everyone looked over at Daniel.

'What? I didn't do anything I just helped her with the rackets.'

'Daniel, what's going on, is there something you haven't told me.' Elizabeth asked.

'No, no I tell you everything, it's just the way they're looking at me that's freaking me out.' Elizabeth smiles and carries on talking.

'Well in any case, I think that Vincent is going to be in my father's office at two this afternoon.'

'How are we suppose to get there Elizabeth, the school only comes out at two.' Milan said smartly.

'Well . . ., we are just gonna have to leave early.'

'What do you mean, escape?' James laughed

'No, I'll ask for permission.'

'How are you going to do that?' Melanie asked with no hope.

'You'll see. Who is our weakest teacher at Dales High?' Elizabeth smiled, and then put the last tomato in her mouth.

'Cat Damien' Milan smiled.

'Yes and where's our class after lunch?'

Everyone nodded excitedly, and then the bell rang. They all got up and started to walk out of the restaurant to the school hall and to Mrs. Damien's classroom.

'Do you even think that Mrs. Damien would fall for it?' Milan asked.

'I'm sure she will.' Daniel said with support.

Elizabeth, Milan, Daniel and Dylan entered Mrs. Damien's class room.

'Elizabeth, I hear that you are going to London in three months time to visit your family.' Mrs. Damien said in a calm and gentle voice.

'Yes we are going to London Mrs. Damien. Well, my dad wants me at Storms Corp. early, I wonder if it is possible for my friends and I, to leave earlier today, say around about half-past twelve.'

'It's still fifteen minutes to half-past. OK sure, but until half-past you carry on with your work.' Mrs Damien replied and turned to the blackboard to write down the work she wanted the class to do for homework.

# CHAPTER 3

# STORMS CORPORATION

## ON THE WAY TO STORMS CORP.

Dark grey clouds appear on the east of Johannesburg. Very low sighted and dimmed by nature's force. Elizabeth and her friends walk towards her father's worldwide corporation. Cars stood in line trying to get to their wanted destination, blowing hooters and chatter of people walking on the side path of the street.

Daniel looked over at Elizabeth, who was talking to Milan, Melissa and Mia. James, Clayton and Miguel were planning to play a prank on some school friends. Daniel moved over to Elizabeth as Milan, Melissa and Mia moved away and walked next to James, Clayton and Miguel. Daniel are finally ready to spoke, but as he was about to open his mouth, they all started to laugh behind him, they stopped and Daniel began to speak again.

'So, um . . . why do you think that Vincent is going to be there, Elizabeth?' Daniel asked looking to the front.

'I don't know . . . I guess it's my instincts telling me it's Vincent.'

'Your instincts?' Daniel laughed, and Elizabeth started to laugh, she stopped when she heard Milan calling from behind.

'Hey, Elizabeth do you think Vincent is cute?' Milan asked, while the others listened. Daniel stopped laughing and looked over to Milan, as she moved over to Elizabeth and Daniel.

'What's the time, Dan.' Milan asked.

'The time is 12:50pm.' he said pettishly.

Milan looks at him vaguely and went to walk next to the others again.

'I think it is just around the corner here.' Elizabeth said excitedly.

'Elizabeth, your father said it's a huge company, and we would be able to see it.' Milan said knowingly

'Yes, we would, but we can't see it now, because this building is blocking our view.' she said plainly.

Daniel looked in the other direction, hoping to find something that will change the subject.

'Err . . . have you heard anything from TL?' he asked quickly.

'Yes, I have but it is between us, and it will stay between TL and me.' Elizabeth stated her reason, as they walked around the corner when they see Storms Corporation, two hundred and thirty floors, all the windows were black paned. The entrance had a black carpet with gold initials at the bottom, and golden doors with the full name on top. Elizabeth and her friends approach the revolving door, with a moral sense they could see Storms Corp. Agents walking around and some talking on their phones.

'Come on, let's go in then.' Elizabeth said looking around at all of her friends, and then they entered. Elizabeth walked towards the security's desk. The security stood up at their arrival, and began to speak in a deep voice.

'Miss, state your name for the record.' He said, as if he is very bored.

Before Elizabeth could say anything, Milan stepped forward, and began to scold the security guard.

'RECORD, WHAT RECORD MUST MISS STORMS HERE, STATE HER NAME FOR?' Milan shouted angrily. Elizabeth and the others stared at her in awe.

'Milan?'

'TELL ME?'

'Milan?'

'Tell me officer, why?'

'MILAN! For pity sake could you stop shouting, everyone is staring at you.' she said rather disturbed.

'ERR, sorry, carry on with what you are busy with.' Milan said slightly embarrassed, and took a few steps back again.

'Um, Mr. Storms is my father, he owns this company.

'Uh, Elizabeth . . . Mr Storms said you would come. The top floor, the large glass office with seven other tiny glass offices for you and your friends.' he said slowly as he read off a piece of paper, that her father had left him.

'Thanks . . . um' she smiled as she wanted to know the name of the security guard.

'You can call me, Eddie' he smiled at Elizabeth and her friends.

Elizabeth nodded in acquaintance and passed the security guard, as they headed towards the elevator. Daniel looked at his watch.

'We have five minutes.' he stated.

Elizabeth pressed the button to open the elevator doors, and then looked up to see that the lift was only coming from the fiftieth floor. They waited for one minute till the elevator came to the "G" level.

'We are now at level G . . .' the computerized elevator said as the doors opened.'

'Greetings Miss Elizabeth Storms, what level are you going to?' the elevator asked as Elizabeth and her friends entered the golden lift.

'The two hundred and thirtieth level please.'

'Like you wish, Miss Elizabeth Storms.'

'My dad installed my name into the elevator . . . yours as well, no need to worry.' she said not taking her eyes off the monitoring device.

'Code please' the elevator said as it came to a halt.

'Computer does the code consist of numbers or words?' Elizabeth asked wisely.

'Numbers . . ."

'Let me think . . . guys you could help me you know, uh got it 5618!' she spoke loudly.

'Access Denied'

'Elizabeth mixes the numbers up, start from eight.' Milan started to stir.

'OK . . . um 8651.'

'Access . . . Denied'

'Oh come on, I know this one should work, 1865!' Elizabeth said loudly once again.

'Access Granted' the door opened and they all stepped out on the top floor.

'Hey wait a minute, that's when Storms Corp. was established.' she said confused.

'How, did you know the code?' Melissa asked slowly.

'My dad told me to mix it up and make it into a year, when I was ten years old.' she bragged. She then looked to her right and saw the glass office on the other side of the room, with eight smaller glass offices leading along to make a corridor.

'There, there's his office.' Daniel pointed.

'Come, lets go.' as Elizabeth approached the office, she sees someone she recognizes and stops dead in her tracks.

Milan her best friend collided into her and made a disturbance to the other agents who were going over their missions united with confidence and certainty.

'OW, jeez Milan look where you're going.' she said after they had fallen to the ground.

'Well, why did you stop then?' Milan asked loudly.

'Um, I thought of something and I didn't realized that I stopped, sorry.' she replied as they got up.

'Now who in the world does not realize when they stop?' Milan said as they started to walk again.

'MILAN! Stop it; you're not helping at all.' Elizabeth yelled

Milan glared at her, as Daniel stepped in between them to stop them from making the situation worse.

'Stop it . . . Both of you. Elizabeth and Milan, you are best friends, and fighting, it's unbelievable.' Daniel said. Mr. Storms stepped out of his glass office. The guard and Elizabeth father's PA escorts Vincent to the elevator. The PA walks in front to the elevator to open it, Elizabeth glares at Vincent "blond hair and hazelnut eyes" when he passes her, he grabs her arm.

'Don't you dare look at me like that missy?' Vince shouted

'Ouch, you're hurting me.' she says. The guard who was with them grabbed him on the arm and dragged him into the elevator.

'Don't you touch her like that ever.' the PA said calmly standing next to him. Vincent growled at him madly, he steps back quickly against the elevator wall, and the elevator doors close.

'Elizabeth, are you okay?' Jeff asked concerned.

'Yes I'm fine dad.'

'Hey, wait a minute what are you doing here so early?' he asked while he looks at his watch, then looks back at his smiling daughter.

'I knew it, I knew that would happen. How did you persuade the teacher to let you go early?' he laughed

'Can't tell dad, it's a secret.' Elizabeth laughs.

Her father's smile disappears and he changes the subject.

'I'll give you a tour of the top floor only, the other floors you have to discover for yourselves.' her dad laughed. Elizabeth and her friends enjoyed the tour; Jeff first showed them the clothing and spy gear.

'Go on grab what you want, and learn to use it within a few weeks.' Jeff ordered them.

Milan was the first to step forward, and then the others followed. Elizabeth smiled at her father, and finally steps forward to take a few things for herself. Elizabeth's father starts to speak.

'You all have the spy gene, did you know that.'

'Spy what?' Milan asked surprise

'Spy gene, it's something you all share.'

'Excuse me; are you trying to say we are all related?' James asked.

'No!' he laughed.

'Then, what do you mean?' Elizabeth asked

'The ability to spy without being seen, Next room.' he said and led them to the microchip office.

'Why are they so small?' Milan asked interested.

'Well when you're comfortable working here, that's going to be injected into you. Elizabeth had hers injected when she was just a baby, no matter where she is I'll find her. The only thing that will make it break will be Hydronite, one injection and the microchip is destroyed' he is suddenly interrupted by Milan.

'THAT! No way . . .' Milan yelled as Elizabeth closed her eyes and smacks her forehead.

'What is Hydronite?' Daniel asked.

'It's a thick blue liquid that you'll only find here. And it does absolutely nothing to the body, it just finds the microchip beacon and destroys it.' he explained.

Her father turned around to see his PA approaching from the elevator. He stands in front of the door, and signals his father to come to him.

'I'll be back.' he said. Elizabeth follows him quietly when he left the room.

'Where did you take him?' Jeff asked.

'He's in our cells on the sixth floor.' he replied.

'Hey, what's going on?' Elizabeth asked who was now standing behind her father.

'Uh, a few things you need to know, about this business . . . don't chip in!' her father said seriously.

'Elizabeth, call your friends I want to show you to your offices.' her father said.

Elizabeth nodded and walked away.


'Come on, guys my dad is going to show us our offices.' she said with a broad smile across her face. Elizabeth's father and William leaded them to their own offices, Elizabeth and her friends sent emails to each other until it was finally time to go home.


It was already 8pm and the Storms family are busy eating dinner.

'You're quite a good cook dad.' Elizabeth smiled.

'Oh . . . Thank you Elizabeth.'

'Where's William?' she asked.

'He left for New York, quarter to twelve.'

'And where's mom?' Elizabeth asked.

'In Cape Town doing business, after that she'll be in Knysna.' he replied, and then the phone rang. Elizabeth's father picked it up.

'Hello Storms residence. What? I'll be right there.' he said in shock.

'Dad, what's going on?' Elizabeth asked quickly.

'Listen I need you to phone a couple of your friends to stay over tonight and make sure that Jon knows they're coming.'

'OK, but could you tell me what's going on?'

'Sorry, Elizabeth I'll let you know in the morning.'

Her father grabs his coat and rushes out the door, she could hear the car start, and pull out of the drive way. Elizabeth drops her fork, and walks over to the phone.

# CHAPTER 4

## SECRET PASSAGE

Elizabeth looked in the mirror on the wall at the telephone. She picked up the handset and dialled Milan's number. It's started to ring.

'Don't worry I'm sure he'll tell me, when he comes back. He's going to the airport most probably.' Elizabeth thought without a smile, also worried and confused, but hid it from her expression in the mirror Elizabeth looks away from the mirror, and out the window. Milan finally answers.

'Hello?'

'Hello, Milan it's me Elizabeth. Um, my father decided to give me a slumber party, so could you let Mia and Melissa know about it and then come over, I'll see you in half-hour.' she acted excitedly.

'Sure, Elizabeth that's great!' Milan replied.

'Bye then.' Elizabeth said.

'Bye.' Milan said and hung up the phone.

Elizabeth placed the handset down and picked it up again, then dialled one. Jon at the outside gate picked up.

'Hi, Jon my friends are coming over for a slumber party. So could you open the gates for them and let them in?' she asked.

'Yes, Miss Storms.' he replied. And he put the phone off. She walked over to the living room sat down on one of the sofas and picked out one of the gadgets she got from the company, and looked at it with curiosity.

'What do you do with this?' she asked herself. She then took out a small booklet manual and read.

'You simply hold this device in front of a locked door, and press the red button, and the door will unlock, if you press the blue button the door will lock instantly.' she looked at it again.

'Wow that is awesome . . . "The Lock Organizer"' she said to herself.

Elizabeth gets off the sofa. She walks towards the living room's door and closes it. Elizabeth points out the Lock Organizer towards the door keyhole and presses the blue button a little red light appears and the sound of a door locking echoed through the living room. Her eyes widen and she presses the red button. Elizabeth turns the handle and it opens.

'Oh, that's how it works? She told herself walking over to the sofa and falling onto it, the puffy sound when she fell blew wind and a breeze blew through her hair.

The next moment the phone rang and Elizabeth jumps up and runs to the kitchen to pick up the phone.

'Hello.'

'Elizabeth, they are here.'

'OK, thank you Jon.' Elizabeth replied. 'You can let them in.'

'Sure' he replied.

Elizabeth hung up and looked out the living room window and very soon saw lights in the driveway, she hears three doors slamming, and she walked towards the front door. She opens the door before Milan could ring the bell.

'OH.' she said and turned around waving goodbye to her father. The car turned around and Milan's father drove down the driveway out the gate. Elizabeth closed the front door after her friends entered.

'Come on.' she said walking towards the steps as they followed her up to her room.

'Hey, Elizabeth where's William?' Milan asked as they reached the top.

'He's in New York doing business for dad.'

'Wow, that's pretty cool, New York!'

'Yeah, and my dad just disappeared out the door tonight too I don't know where he is off to. Elisabeth open her room door and letting Milan, Mia and Melissa in as she follows and closes the door behind her.

Milan put her bag down and walks over to Elizabeth's HI-FI and puts in a CD.

'Who are ready to slumber? LETS GET CRAZY!' she shouted and laughed. The CD start playing the song, it started with camera flashes and Milan posing to each flash and she started to dance when the singer started to sing and very shortly everyone joined in. Two hours later they were painting each others nails, waiting for it to dry and then removing it with nail remover. Elizabeth looked over at the clock on her wall.

'Guys it is half-past ten, there's school tomorrow.' Elizabeth announced.

'You're right, come on guys if I get poor grades at the end of the week, I'm blaming you.' Milan laughed.

'Can you leave the music on, please?' Melissa asked.

Elizabeth walked to her bed and waited for everyone to get into their sleeping bags, she clapped twice and the lights turned off.

## NEXT MORNING

Elizabeth woke up looking around her. Milan, Mia and Melissa were still fast asleep on the floor all around her bed. She removes the covers, gets out of bed walks towards the door, opens it, walks out and closes the door silently. She goes downstairs to the kitchen, gets a bowl from the cupboard and the cereal and sugar from the pantry. She turns around to the fridge and she instantly saw a note on the door.

It read: "Elizabeth, I had to go to work early today. Sorry I just ran out like that last night, something happened in Knysna. When you come to work today I'll explain everything."

'Well OK, that's great to know.' she said opening the fridge door taking out the milk and shutting the door again. She walks to her bowl, and pours the milk into her bowl and then looked over at the clock on the wall. It showed "Half-Past Six." Elizabeth sat down by the dining room table and started to eat her cereal. A few moments later Elizabeth finishes and walks over to the sink to rinse her bowl. By accident she messed some water on her pink silk pj's.

'Oh, damn it!' she shouted, as she leaned forward to try and wash it off, then she heard something like a door opening in a distance. 'What was that?' she asked herself and closed the running tap, and turned around and walked out the kitchen to the passageway.

She saw a door at the end of the passageway.

'That wasn't there before.' she told herself, and walked towards it.

Elizabeth looked up at an armoured door covered in wood panelling so it wouldn't stand out. She looked over at a digital hand-pad, she then looks behind her to see if Pierre was around. Elizabeth placed her hand on the pad and waited for a response before she moves her hand.

'Access granted.' the computer said as the doors opened.

Elizabeth stares down into the passageway, there's a light on each side of the wall. The walls were of grey stone and looked med-evil. She hesitated but walked in anyway as she walks on, she looks up at pictures of her Great Grand Mother and Father, and some other family pictures.

'Why wasn't I told of this?' she asked herself and her voice echoes down the passageway.

As opposed to the lights on each side of the walls, they were black marble and the floor was cold cement. Elizabeth was walking barefoot but never notice how cold it was, because she was anxious to see what was in the next room. Five more steps then she was standing in front of the door which just opened when she approached it. She hesitated but she walked in anyway, she saw three flat screen surveillance monitors but it was not the Storms residence. The first monitor was hallways, the second monitor show the outside and it showed people walking past.

The third monitor showed a room where everything was white and in the middle of the room was a glass pedestal with a brown leather covered book in it. She looked away from the monitors and turned around in a circle to look all around the room. She finally turned towards the monitors again and looked down at the three keyboards.

'OK, this room is high-tech.' she said raising her eyebrows and pressing enter on the middle keyboard. Suddenly she heard an air compressed sound on her left, she turned her head towards it and another door appeared. 'OK, maybe a little simple but high-tech.' she said and walked towards the door and looked all around for a digital hand pad or number pad, but nothing.

'How do I get in here?' she said

'Access denied' the computer said, Elizabeth got a fright and she jumped back when she heard Milan's voice upstairs.

'ELIZABETH, WHERE ARE YOU?' Milan shouted.

Elizabeth didn't hesitate she ran out and the door slammed shut behind her, she ran up the dark passageway to the door where she came through. The door closed automatically and then she ran towards the kitchen and sat down just when Milan walked in.

'Morning' Elizabeth said out of breath but faked a yawn.

'Were you sitting here all the time?' Milan asked, and Elizabeth nodded.

'I have already finished breakfast, I'm just catching a breather.' she smiled. Milan then sat down next to her, she looked up at the clock.

'We're going to be late.' Milan said and got up again walked out the kitchen to the steps and up to Elizabeth's room with Elizabeth right behind her. They enter into Elizabeth's room and she closes the door behind her as Milan walked over to Mia and Melissa shaking them awake. 'Come on guys we're gonna be late.' she said as Melissa shot up and jumped out of her sleeping bag. A few moments later Mia got up and all the girls got dressed.

'Who's taking us?' Melissa asked.

'I think Jon wouldn't mind.' Elizabeth replied.

'So it's with the limo?' she asked excitedly

'Yes.'

'No, I can't take slow cars to school I don't want one bad point for the year.' Milan said waving her index finger around.

'Don't worry Milan, we will get there on time.' Elizabeth laughed.

When they all finished they went downstairs with their school bags where a limo and Jon was waiting for them in the driveway. They walked to the limo and Jon opened the door for them.

'Thank you, Jon.' Mia smiled

'My pleasure.' he replied with a smile as Mia, Milan and then Melissa got in. Elizabeth stopped in her tracks, she had the feeling she has been watched. She turns her head and looked towards the grassy hill outside the estate wall. She saw a man stand with binoculars in his hands, he then put it away and looked down at his wrist. The man disappeared with a bright white light and Elizabeth's eyes widened. Milan, Mia and Melissa didn't notice, but Jon walked over to her.

'What is it Elizabeth?' he asked looking in the direction she was looking.

'There was a man there just a moment ago.' she replied in her accent, and then Jon turned his head to look at her.

'I'll let your father know.' he replied seriously.

Elizabeth nodded and walked towards the limo and got in sitting next to Melissa.

## AT SCHOOL

It was time for break and all the children were running towards the field. Elizabeth and her friends walked slowly to their usual sitting space, under the trees on some steps leading to a closed door. Daniel was nervous but walked over to Elizabeth, he stood dead still in front of Elizabeth, and he started to get butterflies in his stomach when she looked at him. Before Daniel could speak Elizabeth spoke first.

'Daniel can I speak to you for a sec?' she asked.

'Um, sure of course.' he swallowed, she got up and they walked away from the rest of their friends. When they were alone, Elizabeth turned to Daniel.

'Please don't tell the others about this.' she said softly and Daniel nodded. 'I found this secret passageway in my house this morning, and it granted me access. I saw this three surveillance TV screens, the last one I checked, showed this book with an old leather cover.' she said

'Well, maybe you were supposed to see it.'

'Really?' Elizabeth said sarcastically.

'Yeah, my family believes in omen and unnatural signs, my family have a secret business, which I'm not allowed to tell anyone about. I can tell you this, the family business is dangerous. Maybe this means that something is stopping you from seeing it. Daniel tells her with a serious face.

'So they're like ghost hunters.' she asked, changing the subject.

'No, something more unexplainable.' he replied. 'I promised my dad I'd keep it a secret.' Daniel said.

'Oh, is there something you want to ask me?' she asked looking into his eyes, and then he looked towards the field.

'Yes actually there is, Elizabeth, would you like to go to the Spring Ball with me?' he asked quickly, and sigh relieved that he finally popped the question.

'Um, Daniel someone already asked me.' Elizabeth said with disappointment

'Who?' Daniel asked simply.

'Shane Ron.' she looked over to the field where the boys were playing rugby. 'I think that was really sweet of you to ask me to the ball. Shane sort of asked one of his buddies to come and ask me out for him. Which I thought was very amusing.' she laughed, and Daniel had no choice but to laugh along.

Daniel moved aside and let Elizabeth walk first towards their friends, he fall in next to her. They just sat down when Milan, Mia and Melissa burst out laughing, pointing towards Samantha who seemed to be alone outside the school cafeteria, where some boys sprayed her wet with a hose pipe, then the rest of them burst out laughing as Samantha's friends came running to her and escorting her to the bathrooms, trying very hard not to laugh. One of the reporters from the school newspaper took photos. The bell then rang and on the way to the classroom all they could talk about was Samantha's embarrassment.

# AFTER SCHOOL AT DANIEL'S HOUSE

'Did you bring clothes?' Milan asked as they approached Daniel's house gates, where two Doberman Pinchers are barking at them.

Elizabeth's house was as big as Daniel's; there are only more trees and a swimming pool.

'Down boys . . . Kin, Hinchey down!' he shouted, and the dogs yielded, and lay down at the point where they entered the driveway to the front door. They walked into the living room where Daniel's brother, Chris was watching a movie with his girlfriend.

'Come on.' Daniel whispered, as they all went up stairs. 'Girls you can dress in the spare bedroom and guys in my room.'

A few moments later everyone was waiting for Milan downstairs. Minutes later Milan comes stomping down stairs with a mini skirt and leggings a white top with a pink three quarter jacket and black high heels.

'Who would have thought a nerd like you can dress up like that?' Miguel smiled as he looked at her from head to toe.

'Well I have my vice, do you have one?' Milan smirked at him as Elizabeth giggled softly.

'Ooh ouch.' Daniel laughed patting Miguel on the back, turned around and walked through the living room and towards the front door as everyone followed him out, and he shut the door. They all walked towards the gate when Daniel's brother opened the door.

'Daniel, I got another case, I want you to come with me.'

'Oh come on Chris. What if I get hurt again like the last time and walked towards him pushed him into the house and shut the door.

Elizabeth was staring at the house but all she could hear was mumbling, the next moment Daniel comes out of the house and walks to them as Chris peers out the door.

'I can guarantee you, you won't get hurt, I promise.' he smiled and closed the front door.

Daniel didn't even look back, he didn't look at Elizabeth. He opens the gate, and walked out as everyone followed silently. Everyone wondered what Daniel and his brother was talking about.


## AT STORMS CORPORATION

They reached the top floor the elevator doors open and everyone was still quiet. They all went and sat down in their compartment offices, outside Elizabeth's father's huge glass office. When Elizabeth finished her homework she stood up and looked towards her father's office but he wasn't there. She then sat down slowly again, Daniel was sitting in the compartment office next to her.

'I'm sure he's gonna come, Elizabeth.' he said rolling his chair out, and then talking to her. 'Any minute he's going to come from that elevator.' he finished then pointed towards the elevator.

'Daniel, can you please tell me what you and your brother were talking about.'

'Sorry, I said it's a secret, and I have to keep my promise.' he nodded.

'But you can tell me.' she begged.

'No I can't, If Milan hears about this she's going to tell the whole school.' he whispered and wheeled his chair back into his compartment office and Elizabeth rolled her eyes. At that moment the elevator opened and her father walked out with a few of his co-workers following him. Elizabeth stood up again and he looked at her and nodding, signalling her to come to his office. She left her stool and walked to his office as his two co-workers went their separate ways. Elizabeth followed her father in his office and closed the door.

'You said on the note you will tell me.'

'No, you go first. I heard about the controversy at home. Jon said the alarm went off in the house round about seven am. He also told me about the man you saw in the grass hill outside our wall.'

'I found the secret passageway. A man was standing there, when we left for school and the next moment he disappeared with a white light.'

'You . . . you found the passageway? Oh well that's fine. We couldn't exactly get the man you were talking about, but we will. Now why don't we get back to what I was going to tell you . . . ? William's fine, Mom is fine, but she was involved in a car accident in Knysna.'

'What!' she said shocked.

'I know, but she's OK. She just broke an arm.'

'Dad you know how difficult it is for an arm to heal at mom's age. Biology page 134. Are you sure she's OK?' she asked concerned, he nodded.

'We're leaving tomorrow, I already organized it with your teachers.' he said. Rain started to platter on the windows.

Elizabeth then got up, and walked out to her office and sat down. Daniel then wheeled out his chair.

'Psst, what did he say?'

'Sorry it's a secret.' she faked a smile. Daniel then wheeled his chair in again.

It was time to go home, and all of Elizabeth's friends had already left. She waited for her father and they left too.

## AT HOME

'You better go to bed early tonight.' he said sipping his last bit of coffee and walked out of the kitchen to the library. A few minutes later Elizabeth goes to the library.

'Good night dad.'

'Night, my caterpillar.' he smiled.

Elizabeth walked to the stairs and then up to her room, and closed the door, walked over to her bed and just fell on it. She fell asleep immediately, due to the excitement of the day.

# CHAPTER 5

## KNYSNA

The next morning Elizabeth wakes up and she's definitely late for school. She came down stairs still dressed in her pj's and walks into the kitchen; she sat down by the table, her Father walks in and sits beside her.

'Honey we're going to Knysna this morning, I've already arranged for a flight to leave at 11:00 am.' he said slowly

'What about William?' she asked

'No, he's in New York returning the chip, with very tight security. Pack your things it's 9:30, and it's an hours drive to the airport from here.' he said worriedly, he looked away from his watch.

'Dad what are we flying in?' Elizabeth asked.

'The SC Jet of course, now go and get your things.' he replies

'OK, I'll get my things.'

Elizabeth gets up and walks down the long passage, up the stairs and into her room. Fifteen minutes later she steps into the kitchen with two bags full of clothes.

'We're not going to the Bahamas . . . only one.'

'But why dad, a girl needs to stay fresh.'

'No buts Elizabeth, Jon already has the car ready. And I don't think there will be space for two bags.' he said firmly

'Fine then.' Elizabeth said as she dropped the one bag on her left. 'I'm ready.' she smirked

Elizabeth and her father walked out the door to find Jon standing at the door of a new Audi TTi, Elizabeth and her father drive out of the drive way heading for the airport.

'What about school?' Elizabeth asked

'I already phoned the principle and told him we're going to Knysna.'

'Did the guards tell you what happened yesterday morning?'

'Yes, I know, they were trying to break in.'

'Did they tell you he disappeared into thin air, and all that was left was a blue ring?'

'They got it right to break into "McKnight's" house, but why didn't they just teleport them selves into the strong room.'

'Dad who's McKnight and what is a strong room?'

'You'll know in time dear.' he said while he turns in at the airport's entrance.

'Hi, I'd like two ticks to go to the PW Airport, and I'd like to go on my SC Jet please.' he said in a hurry, the booking clerk looked up and back down again.

'OK, thank you mister . . . ?'

'Oh Jeff Storms if you please.' he smiled

The booking clerk looked up slowly and smiled back.

'Certainly, Sir your jet will be ready to go in five minutes.'

'Thank you.' he replied

Elizabeth and her father were about to walk away when the booking clerk started to speak.

'Don't you have an open job for me sir, I really hate this standing . . . it's not my thing, please' she begged

'I'll let you know,' Jeff looks at her name badge. 'Ann Petersen' he smiles and she smiles back.

'But wait don't you need my number?' she asked

'Nope I already have it' he replied

Ann smiles and goes on lunch.

Elizabeth and her father are getting into the jet, the doors close and Elizabeth buckles herself in. Her father just came back from the pilot's cockpit.

'Elizabeth are you buckled in?'

'Yes dad, do you really have her number?'

'Well, technically not and technically I do have her number.' he replied. Elizabeth laughs.

A few minutes later they land at PW airport, the jet finally comes to a stop. Elizabeth looks out the window, she sees reporters waiting for them.

'Dad, what are they doing here?'

'Who?' he replied

'Look!' Elizabeth pointed out the window, her father walked towards her and the window, and then he looks outside.

'They must have heard we're coming, to see mum.' he said.

He stepped back to his seat and picked up his jacket and walked to the jet door. Elizabeth got up and followed, once they got down the jet's steps the photographers started to take pictures and ask questions. They walked really fast to a limo standing ready for them. Elizabeth got in, and moved up to make space for her father, he closed the door and they drove off to the hospital.

The limo stops in front of the hospital door; Elizabeth and her father get out, and walk inside together.

'Hi, I'm Jeff Storms, we have someone that's being held here, Lizzie Storms, she's my wife.' he said

'The other receptionist told me to keep my eyes open for you, your wife is in room fifteen.' she smiles.

Elizabeth and her father walk in the direction that the receptionist is pointing, they finally find room fifteen and stand at the door to see the nurse giving Lizzie, her lunch.

'Oh, honey, Elizabeth what are you doing here? I didn't expect to see you until tomorrow.' she laughed surprised.

'Yeah, well we couldn't wait to see you, right Elizabeth.' Jeff smiled at his wife, the nurse walked out the room, Elizabeth and Jeff walked in and stood either side of Lizzie's bed.

'Hi, mum.' Elizabeth smiles, she went to sit down on a chair at the left of her mother's bed.

'Hi, Elizabeth how's the company treating you, and how was your first day of work, sorry I missed it.' she smiles.

'It was great, and I don't mind . . . really. Mum tell me what happened?' Elizabeth asked, looking concerned

'Oh, honey are you sure you want to hear it?' she replied

'Yes I know for sure that the car hitting you on your right hand side wasn't an accident.' Elizabeth said knowingly.

Jeffrey looked over to Lizzie and she exchanged looks back to Jeff, then she turned back to Elizabeth.

'You're right honey, it wasn't an accident. It was a high speed chase, on the highway but there were barely any cars on the highway. I had this feeling that I was being followed by someone. When I looked in my rear view mirror I saw a black Mercedes right behind me.' Lizzie explains.

'Could you see who was sitting in the driver's seat?' Elizabeth asked.

'No, but I did speed up a little, that's the first mistake I made. When you think you're being followed, you mustn't run.' she pointed out. Elizabeth nods. 'Anyway I was on my way to a secret government meeting, so I'm trying to shake this person off, then

I lost control of the car and the car skidded on it's right hand side on the road, and I guess I'll never know who the driver is, because I passed out. When I woke up, I was laying in a hospital bed with your father at my side.' she looks over at Jeffrey and smiles.

'Hey mom, do you think when we get back, that you and daddy could promote me, and my friends to agent training.' Elizabeth asked with an exciting voice. Her mother smiles at her and then replies.

'We'll see what we can do, but when we get back.' she said seriously, looking at Elizabeth with her eyebrows rose. Elizabeth nodded quickly and accepts her mother's answer.

## MILAN'S HOUSE

Its afternoon in the uptown suburbs and a private loft is in sight, and through a window you could see two of Elizabeth's friends Milan and James. Getting information on the web for the project they need to hand in tomorrow at school.

'Are you sure we're off from Storms Corp. today, Milan? Where's Elizabeth anyway I don't see her coming down the street.' James said looking out the window.

'Yes, and I phoned her house today, they went to Knysna, so you can stop look out the window, Fabio.' James turned away from the window to look at Milan.

'This project's important how could she go to Knysna? James said in an annoyed voice.

''Cause her mum's there that's where the accident happened, Identity Ten T.' Milan pointed it out.

'Oh, I wonder how Daniel and the others are doing on their projects probably further than us, we haven't even got started.' James complained.

'Oh, shut it!' Milan said in a funny English accent.' in a distance you could hear James's brother Sean call out to him.

'James! Mom's calling you for lunch.' Sean shouted from Milan's house driveway.

James looked out the window and shout at his brother. 'Tell her I'm coming!'

'No you'd better come now; mom's already talking to herself!' Sean said with a weird sound to his voice letting James know what that means.

'Bye Milan, see you tomorrow.' he looked at Milan as he picked up his bag and left her alone in her room. Milan got up from her computer desk and walked to the window.

'Bye, James!' she shouted 'Hello Sean, bye Sean!' she continued.

'What are you doing here again?' Sean asked his brother

'A school project, Sean that's what I told mom, but obviously she doesn't want me to study with Milan, instead she wants me to study with Elizabeth, but Elizabeth's not here which I found out a few minutes ago, Milan told me she's in Knysna so I had to work with her.' James explained to Sean

'OK, hold up, nerd, so what you're trying to say is you have a crush on Milan?' Sean asked mysteriously.

James looked over at his brother and pushed him in the bushes next to the driveway, when suddenly Milan yelling from her window to them.

'Wait! James, help me get the others together, I have an idea!'

'But Milan, lunch!' he shouted, then looks at Sean, who is still trying to get out of the bushes.

'Your duty calls.' Sean said teasingly.

'I don't care!' James replied.

'Is that why you're so thin, because you don't care about lunch?' James asked Milan.

'Is that why you have a six pack?' Milan asked rudely. 'Now call them, and Sean can't you tell your mom, James will be a little late for lunch.'

'I want to go with.' Sean said folding his arms.

'Oh, why did I get the feeling you'd ask that?' she asked him.

'So we're good?' Sean asked, smiling.

'Yes, James please I'm serious, give everyone ten minutes to pack!'

'Where we going?' he asked her just when she was about to run to her closet.

'To Knysna!' she shouted back.

## HOTEL ROOM

Its three thirty in the afternoon, Elizabeth and her father, are both in the kitchen serving up a snack for them. They then went to the dining room and sat down at the table.

'Dad?' she asked

'Mm?' he replied looking up at her.

'Do you think we could buy a holiday condo here, its so peaceful.' she laughed.

'We'll see what your mother says.' he smiles and stuffs his mouth full of bread and cheese make Elizabeth laugh at him.

Next moment there's a knock at the door, Elizabeth's father gets up and walks towards the door, he opens it and William is leaning against the left side of the wall.

'What did I miss?' he laughed

'Did you get it to him?' Jeffrey asked

'Yes it's safe, in his safe.' William said as he walked into the hotel room.

'Where's Elizabeth?' he asked.

'In the dining . . .''

'I am right here!' Elizabeth shouted.

William looked through the archway into the dinning room and there sat Elizabeth.

'Oh, hi sis where's your friends?'

'They don't know I'm here.'

'No, they do, didn't you get a phone call dad?' his father shakes his head.

'Oh, you will probably still get it; I got two, one from the bank and one from the secret spy services at the airport.'

'What was the one from the bank about?' Jeffrey asked

'Uh, dad it's R1800 per ticket to get on the SC private jet so times that by seven . . . you have massive debt in your name.'

Jeffrey stopped to think for a moment and finally said.

'R12600.'

'Yes dad they put it on the SC bill, they haven't got the right to their money yet.'

'Damn they're smart.' he said to himself

'So let's get this straight, my friends are coming or most probably are already here.'

William and her father looked at Elizabeth and nodded. Elizabeth felt a tinkle of joy in her toes and suddenly started jumping up and down.

'My friends are coming!' Elizabeth laughed and yelled.

'Elizabeth?' Her father yelled. She ignored her father and started to sing.

'I've never seen her so happy in my entire life.' her father thought as he looked at Elizabeth. His phone starts to ring, it's the airport.

'Jeff Storms here.' Jeff answered.

'Hello, Elizabeth's father?'

'Yes?'

'It's Milan, we're at the airport and we haven't got a lift to where ever you are.'

'All seven of you are at the airport?' he asked surprised.

'Yes' Milan said simply

'I haven't got a car that would accommodate all of you.' he replied

'Uh, dad I've already sent a limo, they have to look out for a man holding a sign saying, E.F.' William interrupted his father.

'E.F.?' Jeff asked with a frown. William nodded. 'OK, William said he already sent a limo it's waiting for you in front of the airport entrance, there's a man holding a board which says E.F, you can ask him to bring you to the 'The Phoenix Inn' Jeff explained to Milan.

'Alright I will do it, Mr. Storms.' Milan said and hung up the phone.

'Dad was that Milan?' Elizabeth asked

'Yes, they're on their way.' he replied

# A FEW MINUTES LATER

Elizabeth, William and their father walked into a store nearby the hotel, they bought all kinds of snacks, to have a mini party when they get back to the hotel. They got to the fruit section when suddenly someone called Jeff's name.

'Jeff? What are you doing here?' the man asked

'Alaster, what are you doing here? Should I ask?'

'I'm here on holiday with my son, Jeff this is John . . . John this is Jeff, this is his daughter Elizabeth, and his son William.' Alaster introduced them. While Elizabeth was staring at John, and he's staring back at her smiling.

'Well, a handsome fellow isn't he?' William whispered into his sister's ear.

'Yes he is!' Elizabeth said out loud

'We'd better go.' her father said, they turned around and walked away.

'Do you think she likes you?' Alaster asked his son.

'Yeah definitely.' he smiled sheepishly.

'Johnny, snap out of it.' Alaster said as he snapped his fingers.

'What? I think I might be interested in her.'

'No you're not, remember, you're gonna use her. Stick to the plan!' he whispered crossly.

'Right, you're right.' he replied 'Sorry' he finished.

'Daddy who is he?' Elizabeth asked while she puts the first item on the counter for the cashier.

'He's a special agent just like William.' he replied

'Oh, he's special alright.' Elizabeth said with a dreamy smile. 'Elizabeth stay away from him.' William ordered.

Elizabeth glared at William, while the cashier rung the next item.

## AT THE AIRPORT

Elizabeth's friends are all inside the limo. They were all laughing and making jokes, they finally reached the front doors of the "Phoenix Inn", and Elizabeth was waiting in front for them. Elizabeth starts to get excited and jumps up and down at the site of all her friends stepping out of the limo; she ran towards them and hugged every single one of them.

'It's so good to see you guys, all of you.' Elizabeth cried.

'Milan, Melissa and Mia, come on guys I wanna tell you something.'

The three girls followed Elizabeth up the stairs into the hotel room.

'I met this hot guy today; apparently he works for my father.' Elizabeth's friends sit open mouths as they listen to this news.

'And that's not all he's a special agent, but he's on holiday with his father.' she finished.

Milan couldn't hold it anymore.

'What's his name?' she burst out.

'John!' Elizabeth laughed.

Next minute Elizabeth's phone rang, Milan, Melissa and Mia picked up their phones and answered their phones at the same time. They all looked at Elizabeth and smiled foolishly.

'Hello, Elizabeth here.' and on the other side of the phone she heard someone with an English accent.

'Hello is this Elizabeth.'

'Yes this is I said my name.' she said cheekily.

'Your father said I could reach you on this number.'

'Who is this?' she asked

'Uh, it's Danny Redburn; your father said that you're my number one fan.'

Elizabeth sat down on the left side of the bed next to Milan in total awe.

'Danny Redburn, yes . . . I thought you were some kind of prankster.'

Milan exchanged looks with Melissa and Mia.

'Wow! I thought you would never phone me . . .' Elizabeth was interrupted by him.

'I'm sorry, I was too busy. I would like to meet you sometime tomorrow in Knysna.'

'Yes of course where?'

There was no answer, they're cut off. She hung up the phone. 'Forget John.' she thought smiling.

# CHAPTER 6

# DANNY REDBURN

Elizabeth woke up the following morning early. She sat up and looked around the room, and saw all her friends laying on the floor in her hotel room, with extra blankets and pillows that were especially brought for them. She sat and thought for a while, and then she remembered that she had to meet the guy of her dreams at The Garden Route Centre. She jumped out of bed with a jolt and ran to the shower, her feet stomping on the hardwood floor. She got in the shower after she opened the taps. Next moment the door opens, and Elizabeth did not hear anything or see anything, her eyes were closed as she was washing her hair. It's Daniel, he didn't notice anything either, so he sat on the toilet. He finally came to his senses, and saw someone standing in the shower and realized it was Elizabeth. He got up from the toilet and pulled up his pants, without thinking he flashed the toilet. Daniel saw Elizabeth stood completely still, and then she finally spoke.

'Milan is that you?' Elizabeth asked, carrying on with her hair. When Elizabeth didn't hear an answer she opened the door as Daniel quickly turned around to face the wall.

'Dan?' she asked.

'If you're ready to get out, just say so, then I'll leave.' Daniel said apologetic. He suddenly hears a soft laugh behind him with the shower still running. Elizabeth had a towel rapped around her body. But Daniel didn't budge.

'Don't be silly, I have something rapped around me it's called a towel.' she said simply.

But when Daniel still didn't look around, Elizabeth walked around him, and stood in front of him.

'Daniel, please pretend I'm your sister . . .''

'Yeah, well that's even more awkward. Elizabeth you are the school's Prima girl and any guy would kill to be in this picture, and I don't want to die.' Daniel said with a serious voice.

'Yeah but you're the Prima guy of our school and any girl would totally cat scratch me, and I don't want any scratches on me. So it will be our little secret, please.' Elizabeth takes Daniel's hands hold them in hers.

'Look.' She said. Daniel finally opened his eyes; there was another awkward moment, while the shower water was still running.

Elizabeth still had shampoo in her hair and it smelled good. Daniel looked at Elizabeth.

'Will you please get back in the shower.' he whispered.

Elizabeth walked slowly back to the shower and got in the shower with the towel still around her, as soon as she closed the door she threw the towel over the door.

Daniel left, and closed the door behind him. Everyone else was still sleeping. Daniel got back into his sleeping bag, and laid with his arms crossed underneath his head, staring into the ceiling, and couldn't get his mind off of what had happened in the bathroom.

Five minutes later, the bathroom door opens and Elizabeth comes out fully dressed in a yellow summer dress and designer flip flops, with the towel that's draped around her head.

Daniel sat up, when Elizabeth sat down on the bed.

'Where are you going?' he asked

'I feel like going to "The Heads" by myself, you know, alone time.' she said 'and then I'm gonna meet someone for lunch . . . you're welcome to come with me.' Daniel nodded.

'Yes, I'd like to, who you're meeting?'

'Danny Redburn.' she replied without hesitance.

'Danny . . . as in the singer Redburn?' Daniel asked astonished.

'Yeah isn't it great I get to meet a super rock star right here in Knysna.' she said with excitement, got up and walked towards the room door trying not to trip over anybody.

'Aren't you coming.' she finished.

'Daniel nodded and got out of his sleeping bag, trying not to wake anyone up, as soon as he stood up straight he saw James's eyes looking at him and holding two thumbs up. Daniel walked towards the door, he saw Elizabeth sitting at the breakfast table, and someone serving her breakfast. He closed the room door behind him and sat down next to Elizabeth, but as soon as he sat down a bowl of oats cereal was put down for him.

'When we're done eating you and I can leave.'

'Sorry I haven't actually asked, what is "The Heads"?' Daniel asked.

'Haven't ever been to Knysna before?' Elizabeth laughed. Daniel then shook his head.

'I always came here as a child on holiday with my parents, my brother was always out on missions, but he somehow always got it right to surprised us, and "The Heads" was always the place I wondered off to.' she said calmly as she put a spoon full in her mouth.

'Well, OK I would like to see it then.'

'Oh, it's beautiful, you'll love it.' she swallowed her last bit of cereal, as Daniel laughed.

## A FEW MINUTES LATER

Elizabeth was waiting in front of her father's bedroom door, he was out to the hospital, to fetch Elizabeth's mother. Daniel was inside dressing into day clothes.

'Are you done yet?' Elizabeth asked impatiently.

'Yes just one sec.' he replied.

Elizabeth laughed.

'One.' she counted and opened the door. Elizabeth's mouth flew open at what she was seeing, she then walked into the room towards Daniel, and he was still busy pulling his T-shirt over his head. Elizabeth held open her hands and placed it over his abs.

'I didn't know you worked out.'

'OK, stop.' he smiled, and pulled his T-shirt down. 'Now I'm ready.' he finished.

'OK, let's go then.' she said, She walked towards the front door, Daniel closed the door behind them.

# THE HEADS

Elizabeth was holding onto a wooden pole, which gave an excellent view of the other side, and down onto the rocky heads. There were tourists everywhere taking pictures of almost everything except Elizabeth and Daniel. He was looking all over the place, down the hill, and to the other side, he saw what seemed to be a separate island, separate from the main land. Daniel heard Elizabeth giggle.

'The last one down is a fart.' Elizabeth laughed

'Oh, no you don't!' Daniel yelled and followed.

They were laughing all the way down to the beach. They raced down the stone steps; Daniel had landed in first place. There seem to be dark green bushes everywhere. There weren't many people around, just a father, mother and their son, splashing each other in the shallow waters.

Daniel and Elizabeth moved to a quieter place. All you could hear was the rushing sound of waves. Daniel looked back and saw the stone steps were quite a distance away. Elizabeth sat down on a rock, she saw the two parents and their son came out the water and went to sit down on a towel. They took a picnic basket and start their breakfast. Daniel finally looked over at Elizabeth and went to sit down next to her, Elizabeth looked over at him.

'These people are nosy, hey.' she whispered 'Come on; I'd like to show you something else before we go back.' Elizabeth said as she got up and pulled Daniel by his hand. She then let go, Elizabeth was walking along the waterside, which finally lead to a small cliff, which was overlooking the ocean. It had a golden shine to it. Daniel looking out over the sea, he could see fishermen with their boats.

Elizabeth turned around to face Daniel.

'Daniel can you promise me one thing.'

'Yes?' he replied.

'You will always be there for me, and save me when I'm in trouble?' she asked looking down, as she came closer, they were 20mm apart.

'Yes, of course I will.' Daniel stood still.

'Cause I have a feeling . . . something bad is gonna happen to me.' she said. Daniel stepped closer and hugged her.

'Will you come with me to meet Danny?' she asked letting go of Daniel.

'OK, sure.' Daniel replied. Daniel turned around and they walked back to the stone steps. Suddenly Daniel and Elizabeth heard Milan's voice shouting from somewhere up the hill.

'Elizabeth . . . Daniel!' she shouted.

They ran up the steps to meet Milan.

'What is it?' Elizabeth asked

'It's your mom, she's at the hotel.' she said excitedly.

Elizabeth started to smile and ran towards the hotel.

'What was happening down there between you and Elizabeth, did you kiss?' Milan asked Daniel anxiously

'NO! No we didn't.' Daniel said.

'Then tell me.'

'She was scared, she had a feeling that something bad was gonna happen to her.'

'When?' Milan asked

'I don't know, but I'd better keep my eyes open.'

'And then?'

'What is it to you?'

'Fine if you don't want to tell me, that's fine.'

'She also asked me if I could go with her to meet Danny Redburn.'

There was a high pitched gasp from Milan.

'I thought he said he wants to meet her alone.' Milan said surprised.

'So you knew.'

'Yeah, well you're the only one of the guys that knows now.' Milan laughed.

## HOTEL LIVING ROOM

Daniel and Milan were walking upstairs to the main door and up another flight of stairs into the hotel room. There's lots of noise, as everyone is cheering and saying hello to Elizabeth's mother. Elizabeth was sitting next to her mother on the arm of the chair.

'Guy's did you know that Mr. Storms and ten constructor workers built this inn, that is why no one knows about it, and another reason why it's so far from the town. So that agents could meet here, and go over their missions together.' Elizabeth's mother said as she looked over at Jeff.

'Mum, guess what?' Elizabeth asked.

'What?' she asked enthusiastically

'I'm going with Daniel to meet singer Danny Redburn in town for lunch.' she said. James, his brother Sean, Clayton and Miguel, all open their mouths and look over at Milan, Mia and Melissa.

'Oh really, well that's great, what's the time now?' her mother asked surprised.

'It's ten forty five.' Daniel said quickly looking up from his watch.

'Why don't you and Daniel walk so long, to where ever he's gonna meet you . . . where is he gonna meet you.'

'He didn't say.' at the same time Elizabeth's phone rang, she answered and it was Danny Redburn.

'Hi, Elizabeth here.' she answered

'Hi, Elizabeth, its Danny can you meet me at Maureen's restaurant in the gardens, or if you want I can ask for privacy.'

'No, I'd rather meet you at the outside tables.'

'Sure OK, see you twelve o'clock.'

'OK, sure, bye.' Elizabeth replied excited, and hung up the phone. 'Dad, something doesn't feel right, going to meet Danny, isn't there something you can give Daniel and me so that you can listen in on the conversation.' she asked

'I think I might have a little something here.' he said and walked over to a wall with paintings of doctors listening in on their patients hearts. He knocked four times on one after the other, and suddenly there was this mechanical sound and the wall flipped slowly to the front, her father pulled out two ear devices, one for Elizabeth and one for Daniel.

'There, put that in you right ear.' Elizabeth and Daniel did so, and then Milan talked.

'Little, you call this little, this looks like pretty much to me.

'Milan.' Elizabeth said irritated, and pulled her long hair over the ear piece. Milan kept quiet after that, and just looked at all the gadgets, and weapons.

'Guys you go help Daniel to get ready, girls you go help Elizabeth.' her mother ordered.

'Uh, before you go, there's something I need you to put in your eyes, it's just like a contact lens, except it has a camera in. Her father gave one to Daniel and one to Elizabeth.

'Dad is this like my first mission.'

'Yes, actually it's sort of a test, to see how you will do in the actual mission.' he pointed out.

'Come on, we only have thirty minutes left.' Daniel said looking up from his watch once again.

Twenty five minutes later, Daniel and Elizabeth came from the room, with their friends following behind them.

'Ear and Eye check.' her mother said looking into Elizabeth's eye and ear, then Daniels.

Elizabeth's father was sitting at his laptop, typing in keywords.

'There, we're live.' he said taking his hands off the keyboard. Elizabeth and Daniel walk towards the laptop; they could see themselves in the screen.

'Now the hearing devices allow you to listen in on each other's conversation but only about 50 metres, so Daniel if he asks you to go away, just do it, go sit in the limo and keep an eye on her from the window.

'OK, what's the time?' he asked

'It's fourteen minutes to twelve.' Daniel said looking away from his watch.

'We're set, and don't worry, I'll have full contact with you, now go Charles is already waiting for you outside. Oh and there is a laptop in the limo, now go.' he said, and Elizabeth and Daniel ran out the room, down the stairs, and got into the limo as fast as they possibly could. The limo drove off.

# MAUREEN'S

Elizabeth and Daniel went into the restaurant gates, and go straight to the area where the outside tables are. Danny sat two tables away from the entrance, waiting for her. She and Daniel walked towards Danny. Elizabeth sat down on the opposite side of the table and Daniel sat down on the right of her.

'Hi, Danny how are you?' she asked

Danny exchanged looks with Daniel to Elizabeth.

'Who's this?' he asked looking back at Daniel.

'I'm . . .' Daniel was interrupted by Elizabeth.

'This is Daniel, my boyfriend.' she said. Daniel looked over at her and then back at Danny and smiled.

'Nice to meet you man.' he said in a skirmish English accent, and faked a smile. The smile turned into a grin.

'Elizabeth, can you tell your boyfriend to go stand over there somewhere, I want to talk to you alone.' he said as he put down his hand after pointing out two tables that are open.

Daniel looked at Elizabeth, and she nodded. Daniel got up and went to sit two tables away from Danny and Elizabeth.

'Elizabeth, it's a pleasure to meet the world's princess.' he said charmingly.

'Well it's a pleasure to meet you Danny.' she smiled.

Danny laughed.

'I heard you have a family heirloom . . . an ancient document. I was asked to be a lead actor in a movie, and the documents play a big part in the story' he said as Elizabeth could hear her father speaking in her ear.

'Elizabeth he's lying, Danny could never act. Well he's not getting that right now either'

'Yes, but I'd rather have the director speak with my father.' she said and looked behind her to Daniel who ordered himself some water.

'I'll tell him to give your father a call, but I'm asking you, do you know about it.' he looked at Elizabeth, who looked back at him and replied:

'No, sorry I only started at my father's company three days ago, he didn't tell me anything about a family heirloom or ancient document, that run in the Storms family, don't you think a fake would work in the movie, and beside you're sounding desperate.' Elizabeth said as she stood up, and walked off to Daniel.

'Come on Daniel, this is the feeling I had this morning. It's gone now, after I pulled off the deal.

They left the restaurant; they got into the limo and drove off.

As soon as they left, Danny pulled his cell phone out of his pocket and dialled a number.

'She knows something's up, meet me tonight behind the hotel, if we take the one most loved, they'll hand it over.' he said and hung up the phone.

'I thought he was sweet, but it seems the bad feeling was about him, that feeling is gone. Thank you Daniel, for being there for me.'

'It's my pleasure.' Daniel smiled, and looked out the window.

'You were great Elizabeth, and Daniel nice distance. You still had an eye on her, you guys should become actors.'

'Thanks dad.' she laughed.

'Yeah, thanks Mr. Storms.' Daniel followed.

A few minutes later they arrived at the hotel, and everyone was standing outside waiting for them, first Daniel let Elizabeth climb out, then he followed.

'AND THE NOMINEE GOES TO, NOT ONE BUT TWO PEOPLE ... ELIZABETH STORMS AND DANIEL SAWTS!' Milan shouted out to them as they came up the stairs.

Daniel received quite a number of pats on his back including Mr. Storms and hugs from all the girls. Daniel sat down on the step.

'Daniel are you not coming?' Clayton asked.

'No, I just need some fresh air.' Daniel said. Clayton turned around and walked with everyone else into the hotel. James's brother Sean came and sat down next to Daniel.

'Hey, that was pretty cool ... Mr. Storms brought up some satellite imagery. Hey, I challenge you to a game of goals, ten each.'

'You're on.' Daniel laughed, and they ran into an open field nearby.

Time flew by quickly, the sun was starting to set, and it was getting darker. Daniel and Sean were still kicking goals. Now and then he would look up to the hotel room that everyone slept in, and Elizabeth was standing by the window watching them play.

'Oh, yeah, that was my fiftieth.' Sean laughed making a little victory dance.

Daniel laughed as he looked back at the window, the light was off, and something told him, something's wrong. He left Sean standing there on his own, with the ball still in the net.

Daniel ran into the hotel room the light bulb was broken, and there was a tissue lying on the floor at the window where she was standing. There was a window that was wide open, he ran towards it. He realized what happened and ran out again. He runs into the living room breathing heavily.

# CHAPTER 7

# THE RANDSOM NOTE

Daniel was looking at everybody in the room and then he ran out the door, down the hotel stairs to the window that's open. He then looked behind him and saw a dark spot in the field: he walked towards it and stood in the middle of it.

'What the?' he said to himself, as he heard Milan's voice.

'Daniel, what's going on?' she asked as she walked towards him, and stood with him in the spot. Then everybody came out including Elizabeth's mother and father.

'Daniel, what is it?'

'Mr. Storms I think something terrible has happened to Elizabeth . . . I think she's been kidnapped.' he said looking up at the window that's open. Mr. Storms didn't move.

'How do you know that?' he said seriously

'Go look for her in her room, Mr. Storms. I'm not lying to you.' he said as Elizabeth's father turned around and walked back into the hotel, with Elizabeth's mother on his heels. A few minutes later Mr. Storms stood at the open window.

'Here's a note' he said astoundingly

Daniel ran into the hotel, to the room. He walked to Elizabeth's father. Jeff handed the note to Daniel. Daniel opened it and read it.

"If you ever wanna see, Elizabeth again, you'd better hand over three million rand. Phone this number for arrangements 076 584 5144"

You'd better write down that number.' Mr Storms said.

Daniel looked back up at Mr. Storms, and he walked over to the tissue lying on the floor. He smelled it.

'Chloroform' he said looking up at Elizabeth's mother.

'Looks like we have a real battle on our hands.' she said as she looked over to Daniel, everybody was still in the field outside.

'Mr. Mrs Storms, I have something to say, this is my entire fault. Elizabeth asked me to protect her from danger that is why she asked me to go with her to meet Danny. She was scared something bad was gonna happen to her, and in the limo she told me the feeling was gone. Now look what happened.' he said pointing out the room.

'We'll help you where ever we can, Daniel.' Clayton said from the door, as he looked behind him. Everybody was now standing there, and then he looked back at Mr. Storms.

'Please, let me and the rest of Elizabeth's friends deal with this mission.' he asked

Mr. Storms stood and thought for a moment, then finally nodded yes.

'But, under one condition, you call me if you need anything.' he said and they ran out the room to the porch in the back, to get their plans in order.

A few minutes later Daniel's phone rang, he answered. Everyone could hear it was his mother.

'Daniel, where are you? All I got was a note on the fridge.'

'Mom . . . I'm fine mom. I'm with Elizabeth's mother and father in Knysna, so calm down.'

'What the hell are you doing there?' she asked

'We're on a company field trip.' he lied

'Well, you could have just told me.' she said in relieve

'Yeah, mom anyway it's great to hear your voice.' he said as he looked over at Milan and the girls who were all laughing at his insight.

'Buy honey look after yourself'

'Buy mom.' he replied, as he hung up the phone, and glared at Milan, Melissa and Mia, who suddenly stopped their silliness.

'OK, what we should do is ...' Daniel was interrupted by Clayton who just came from the room where Elizabeth was captured.

'Daniel, Elizabeth's father said we should head for the private airport and go and meet my cousin.'

'What private airport?' Daniel asked Clayton in an irritated mood.

'He said there's one just down that road' Clayton pointed out the opposite direction from the road that was leading into town.

'There's an airport there but it doesn't show on the map.' Miguel pointed to the map.

'That's why it's private, nobody knows it's here.' Clayton replied.

'I can't explain it to you again we have to go, meet my cousin. Come on!' he said as he walked down the porches steps to the gravel road leading towards the airport.

'We have to walk?' Milan asked in a snobbish manner

'Yeah, Jon isn't here to drive us.' Sean said

'Shut up you pip squeak.' James cussed

'I'm telling mom.'

'How you gonna tell her, when you haven't got a phone.' James said as everyone laughed.

They walked for a half hour until finally they reached the strip.

'Uh, finally we are here.' Mia said.

They walked to a wired gate, opened it and walked in. Suddenly they were stopped by a security guard.

'Can I help you kids?' the security guard asked.

'Yeah, we're going to Harrismith.' Clayton said

'Who sent you here?'

'Uh . . .' Clayton was interrupted by a phone call.

'This is a private airport son, no one is allowed . . ."

'Sorry I got to take this call.' Clayton said and answered the phone.

'Hello, Clayton speaking. Who's this?'

'Clayton, it's Elizabeth's father are you at the airport.'

'Yes, Mr. Storms we're here. Thank very much you bye.

'Bye'

'You're the newbie's at the company, how old are you?'

'Why does our age matter to you, can we just pass please.' Daniel said and walked past the security guard, who had made way.

They walked towards the small office which led up to a control room, they entered the room and there was about three people controlling flights. Clayton stepped forward towards a man just a few years older than him.

'Hi are you, Cristiano Lopez.' this really handsome guy came forward and shakes Clayton's hand, whilst nodding, and Milan, Melissa and Mia's eye's twinkle at the site of Cristiano.

'Yes, I'm from Mexico, nice to meet you, just got here yesterday.' he replied in a Mexican accent.

'He even has an accent' the three girls giggled.

'Um, this is Daniel; he would like to arrange a flight to Harrismith.'

'For all seven of you, wow that's a first'

'Yes.' Daniel replied

'OK, well let's see.' he said. He walked over to some paperwork on a desk, and shoved it all off. 'Sorry it's a bit messy, uh for all seven of you to Harrismith at the same time, would have to acquire a army chopper, which is priceless for Storms Corp. agents, but a fortune for your boss, who's your boss?' he asked.

'Mr. Storms himself.' Milan said.

'Oh, I'll show you the way, follow me.' he said and left the room with the seven of them following him.

'Here's your ride to a small town nobody likes, except its residents. Robert Wilson will take you, enjoy your trip.' He said as he walked out of the chopper housing, took his phone out of his pocket, and dialled a number.

'Hello, yeah they're on their way.' he said and hung up the phone.

'Shall we be on our way then?' Robert asked in an English accent. They all nodded as though they were scared of him but they got in.

'Whoa, hold up!' Cristiano shouted as he came back. 'Mr. Storms would like me to come with you, is that alright with you guys?' he asked.

'Yes!' Milan, Melissa and Mia all shouted at once.

Daniel nodded as Cristiano ran towards the chopper's door and pushed in front of Daniel.

'Buckle Up.' Robert ordered as the blades started whooshing, one of the workers closed the chopper door and ran to stand a sensible distance from it as it wheeled out of the housing. As soon as the chopper was out in the open it lifted up in the air, and Robert converted it forward, to dart to Harrismith as fast as it can go.

# CHAPTER 8

# HARRISMITH

The chopper was now flying through the golden colours of the sun setting.

'Cristiano, we might be there by night fall.' Robert announced. Cristiano nodded.

Once they landed the whooshing sound of the chopper blades seemed to slow down and the dust started to clear.

'Who's that?' Melissa asked when all the dust had finally dropped.

'That's Mike Oren the company's task driver.' Cristiano replied.

'How did he know we were coming?' Milan asked.

'I told Mr. Storms to send him over.' Cristiano hesitated as he opened the door and made way for them.

'Thanks Robert, I appreciate it.

'Cristiano picked up his back pack and left the chopper.

Milan, Mia and Melissa were already in the limo waiting on the six boys.

'What a way to keep cover.' Sean laughed, and James hit him over the head.

'Ouch, what you do that for?'

'Shut up, you wit!' James yelled as everyone else laughed.

Cristiano's phone then rang, and he went back into the chopper for some privacy. James his brother Sean, Clayton and Miguel climbed into the limo except Daniel. He was waiting for Cristiano.

'Daniel get in, it's dark and all you can see are the chopper's lights.' Milan said.

Daniel watched Cristiano walk up the ramp, cell phone still ringing.

'Cristiano speaking here, what's the situation?'

'Cristiano, I have another task for you . . .' a man said on the other side of the phone.

'Alright I'm listening.' he replied.

A few moments later Cristiano came down the ramp again, pulled the ramp up and closed the door. The blades of the chopper started whooshing again.

'Excuse me, Cristiano, we can't go into town with a white limo, don't you think anyone would notice. I'm pretty sure nothing like this has happened in such a small town in years.' Daniel said worried.

'I'm sorry do you have a problem, if I . . ., I mean if Mr. Storms never sent this limo we'd all be walking to Harrismith and you can't do that to the young ladies in the car.' Cristiano replied as Daniel snorted.

'Well let's just set things straight here . . . I Don't Trust You.' Daniel said slowly.

'Listen here you pipsqueak, I've been in this company for four years. So I'm not gonna let someone under my status order me around, I really don't care if you don't trust me. Now! Get! In!' he shouted slowly. Daniel and Cristiano got in, and Mike rode off.

'It is still fifteen kilometres more, sir.' Mike stated.

'Thanks Mike.' Cristiano replied.

So far the road was quiet; it was so silent in the limo you could hear a pin drop. It was new moon and all you could see were the dark shadows of open fields, and trees. Finally they came across the small towns lights.

Is that it?' Milan asked as she laughed.

'Yes, are you disappointed?' Cristiano asked.

'Yeah, Milan I've been here before, and it still looks the same.' Clayton said, as Milan squinted out the window.

'Why is the cross in mid-air?' Melissa asked.

'Well technically, it's standing on the edge of the mountain. It symbolises the crucifixion of Jesus, its twenty four meters long, and fourteen meters wide.'

'My, cousin just lives a little way out of town, maybe we should stay at some hotel or something seeming that you've been here more times than me, and we're all really tired.' Clayton stated.

'Yes, I do know of one place.' he replied as they rode over a short bridge leading into the town's main street. 'Mike you can pull over at the Grand Hotel, for a pit stop. I'll call you again if I need you.' Cristiano finished.

'Yes sir.' Mike replied.

A few seconds later, the white limo stopped and everyone got out, then Mike rode off again.

'After you ladies.' Cristiano said. The girls passed him, and the boys followed.

The inside was all wood. The front desk had a granite topping. There were stairs leading up to the second floor.

'Hello, Kelly.' Cristiano smiled, 'Do I still have my room.'

'Yes, you know where it is.' she replied.

Everyone went up stairs to the room where Cristiano's staying. He opened the door, there was a double bed. With a lot of floor space, you could obviously tell he hasn't been there for a long time.

'OK, everyone take a sleeping bag from the cupboard, and get yourself a space, and get some sleep. Ladies you can sleep on the bed.' Cristiano pointed out, as he got himself a sleeping bag and a space. He then put out the light.


The next morning, Daniel was the first to wake up, with a pain in his back from sleeping on the floor. Then he realized Elizabeth wasn't with them, the next thing he realized was Cristiano wasn't in his sleeping space by the window. Daniel then woke everyone else up.

'Guys . . ., GUYS come on we have to go.' Daniel shouted.

'What day is it?' Milan yawned.

'It's Thursday; Clayton does your cousin work, anywhere?' Daniel asked, as he got up, still in his clothes from the day before. Everyone else also followed and got up; they all slept in their clothes.

'Hey, where's Cristiano.' Melissa asked.

'I don't know.' Daniel replied simply, looking out the window, the sun from the east was shining in his eyes.

A few minutes later everyone was outside, waiting for Sean.

'Honestly who agreed for James's little brother to come along?' Mia asked pulling her face up.

James then pointed at Milan.

'What, ME! He asked if he could.' she replied when the door opened, and Sean stepped out.

Everyone except Daniel was staring at him.

'What?' Sean asked. Turned around and looked at James.

'Just come on.' Daniel said before anyone could complain.

They walked up the main street, until they reached the shops. Daniel went in every single shop but couldn't find Cristiano anywhere.

'What's the time now?' Milan asked and complained. 'It's almost eleven am. Daniel we haven't even had breakfast yet.

'Clayton isn't there a place we could eat.' James sighed.

'No, I'm sorry. But there is a bottle store there maybe they have something for us to drink.' Clayton pointed and they all followed him. They all come out with a cool drink in their hands.

'Let's carry on.' Daniel ordered.

They passed two shops, and then crossed the street from the right over to the left.

'Sean? Come on.' James called. 'This is no time for window shopping.' he finished.

Sean ignored him and James turned around and kept on walking.

Everyone was across the street when, Sean realized they were gone. He looked over the street, and everyone was waiting for him. He started to cross, when suddenly two black cars came rushing towards him. Sean was frozen with fear.

'SEAN!' James shouted and without hesitance James ran.

'James wait!' Daniel shouted, but it was too late.

James was running towards Sean, grabbed him and pulled Sean in the nick of time, out of the way. The two cars had passed. They hit their brakes so hard it echoed in the area. Everyone in the main street was looking at James and Sean, who were still standing in the middle of the street. James was looking at the two cars, who were turning around, then look back at Daniel and the others.

'RUN!' James yelled, as the six of them took off.

'Are you alright, James asked. Sean nodded. 'Come on we have to go.' he finished, and pointing at the two cars who were heading for them again. They ran around the corner and saw Daniel and the others run into a creativity shop. James and Sean stopped and watched as the two cars turned in the opposite direction.

'They went into a shop over there.' James said calmly. They walked towards the creativity shop, where James had seen Daniel and the others enter.

Daniel was the first one to see Cristiano standing at the counter talking to someone, Cristiano and the other person's back was turned to them.

'Hey, heads up.' Daniel whispered, as everyone looked towards the counter.

'Who are you buying for again?' the girl asked.

'Um, my grandmother.' he replied. James and Sean walked in.

'They're gone.' James said as he heard Cristiano's voice.

'She loves knitting.'

'OK, the cheapest wool we got is this.' the shop assistant said as she took out a twenty five gram ball of wool. She had dark brown hair, hazel brown eyes and was tall and thin. Clayton realized who the girl was.

'That's my cousin Emma.' he whispered trying not to let Cristiano hear him.

'How much is it?' he asked, Emma turned around once again.

'Where's the price?' she asked herself laughing.

Cristiano pulled out a gun from his back pack aiming it at Emma. Clayton started to panic.

'Emma!' he shouted, Emma turned around to see Clayton, and a gun aiming right at her head.

Daniel and Clayton tried to stop Cristiano, but he burst right through them, and out the shop's door. Cristiano reached the corner not knowing which way to go, he shot at Daniel and Miguel and missed them by centimetres. He then ran down the street, over the crossing. He ran into two people crossing the street, while Daniel and Miguel took the shortcut.

'He's fast.' Miguel said out of breathe.

The two black cars they saw earlier were racing ignoring the red robot. There were cars parked everywhere but very little people on the pathway.

Cristiano desperately tried to dodge everyone as he looked back at Daniel and Miguel while firing the gun at them. They passed the blue and red post office box, the two cars where still behind them. Daniel and Miguel heard gunshots behind them, as everyone else was ducking for cover and screaming they kept on running. A stray bullet hit Cristiano's leg, and he fell down screaming, dropping his gun. In front of a coffee shop an old man was sitting with a friend drinking coffee.

Daniel approached Cristiano, who was getting up and hit him in the face with his fist.

'What do you know about Elizabeth?' Daniel asked loudly. The two cars passed slowly if nothing was wrong, and Miguel very bravely threw out a cuss sign.

'I know nothing, I swear.' Cristiano said with pain.

'Really, why did you try to shoot Clayton's cousin in the head?' Daniel asked

'She was interfering.' Cristiano shouted as Miguel picked up the weapon from the ground and pointed it at Cristiano.

'What was she interfering with?' Daniel shouted

'An AGP.' he replied

'I'm not a genius. What does that mean?' Daniel asked rudely

'An AGP means A Government Practice.' Cristiano explained.

'Dealing with what?'

'Miguel please call the police.' Daniel ordered and Miguel took out the phone and dialled the number.

'Transportation through a diamond ring, they say she stole their idea.' Cristiano explained further

'I don't know, but it sounds like someone framed her.' said the old man from his table at the coffee shop.

'Thank you. Sir' Daniel said sincerely.

Daniel kicked Cristiano's leg where he was shot, and he screamed in pain.

'Will you hold this man at your custody till the police arrive?' Daniel asked the old man, he nodded and his friend approached Daniel.

'Who are you?' the man asked.

'Nobody important, come on Miguel.' Daniel replied.

'You know this is the first action we've had since World War Two.' the man said.

'Yes, I can imagine.' Miguel laughed and gave the gun to the old man. 'Maybe you know how to work it.' he said and followed Daniel, as the police came around the corner with their sirens flashing.

'Here they come.' Melissa said with excitement, everyone looked up except Clayton and Emma.

'Did you get him?' Milan asked.

'No, they got him.' Miguel replied.

'They?' she asked

'Yeah his own people shot him in the leg how ironic?' Miguel replied.

'It must have been a stray bullet.' Daniel added. 'Emma are you, OK' Daniel asked Emma. She can only nod her head as she was still shocked.

'They were all standing outside the door, when Emma's grandmother came and stood with them.

'Emma, are you alright? Here, you can take the rest of the day off, I never thought anything like this could happen in Harrismith.' she said and handed Emma her wages for the week.

'Six hundred Rand.' Milan laughed. 'We get so much more than that.'

'Oh really, how much do you get?' Emma asked.

'We get three thousand nine hundred a month.' Milan replied, and Emma stood up.

'Well, my life in your world may seem dull, this is just my cover. You won't believe how much money I have in my private bank account.' Emma smiled, though the drama had faded away and she didn't seem to care. 'I've been working for this company for four years now, you do the math.' she finished

Milan smiled and looked over at Mia and Melissa.

'Can we go?' Sean asked

'OK, come I have a car.' she said and walked away from the shop door towards a red pick-up truck.

'This is your car? I expected it to be better.'

'No questions please get in.' she said as the three boys got on at the back.

'In where?' Milan asked

James and Clayton helped the girls to get on the back. Daniel got in the front with Emma.

She started the pick up, and drove off.

# CHAPTER 9

# EMMA STRYDOM

Emma stopped in a light bricked driveway. Three garage doors with a hideous thick brown line. The house was beautiful, the exterior was uneven sandstone. The garden was starting to bloom, seeming it was nearly the end of winter. A beautiful black dog, with a shiny coat came running to the small white gate.

'Is it always cold here?' Milan asked as she got off the back of the truck. Emma then got out, Daniel followed.

'Yes, you'll get used to it. Sort of.' she said rubbing her hands together.

'What's the dog's name?' Miguel asked, putting his hand through the gate to rub the dogs head.

'Thunder.' she replied.

Miguel pulled his hand out again, and turned around to look at Emma.

'What, you can hear him at night but you can't see him. Don't worry I have a cat called Eagle.' Emma laughed as the rest of them got off the back of the truck.

'Let's get inside before you northern people freeze.' Emma said as she opened the small gate where they had stopped, everyone followed her as the dog was in everyone's way. 'Thunder!' she shouted, the dog left them alone. Emma walked towards the front door, and opened it. Everyone follows her in.

'So what brings you here, a field trip?' Emma laughed again.

'No, Elizabeth was kidnapped, and I wrote down the number but never phoned it.' Daniel spoke up before Clayton could.

'Elizabeth, kidnapped? So that would explain my head on the plank. They knew you'd come to me for help, so they sent Cristiano. Did you guys know you had a double agent?' she asked looking at all of them.

'Daniel was very distrustful of Cristiano.' Milan replied.

'No, I knew about Cristiano, I just had to play it safe at the shop. It's someone bigger, and it's obvious you guys don't know who it is. Where's that number?' she asked Daniel, taking out her phone, as Daniel took out his.

'Um, 076 . . . 584 5144.' he replied reading off the phone.

Emma immediately pressed the green symbol on the phone, and put the phone to her ear.

'Its ringing.' she informed them.

## A MOMENT LATER

'Hello, who's this?' a man asked

'This is Emma Strydom, looks like your assassination thingy didn't work, and I am feeling so sorry for Cristiano who by the way is sitting in the county jail.' Emma replied

'That's nice to hear Cristiano's safe, you see we have a friend of you, in fact an even closer friend who would like to speak to you.' he said and held the phone towards Elizabeth and William.

'Speak.' the man said. Emma put her phone on speaker. Everyone heard Elizabeth's voice for the first time today.

'Guys, I know you'll find us, it's a crummy old warehouse . . . no please . . .' Elizabeth begged.

'Don't touch her!' William shouted.

'Listen to me Emma, your phone is being tracked'

'How can that be, my phone is secure.'

'It was an easy hack.'

'Now what?' said a man in a distance.

'Let them come to . . .' the phone was hung up. 'us.' the man said and walked out the room.

'What about them?' the man asked. The other man stopped and turned around.

'I don't know, Johnny, put their socks back in their mouths. So that they can shut up.' the man said, and walked out. Johnny lifted the socks and stuffed it in their mouths.


'That voice it sounds so familiar.' Emma said walking through them, and sitting on a couch.

'Yeah, it's Danny Redburn.' Daniel replied as Emma looked back up at him.

'Danny Redburn, the actor Redburn.' Daniel nodded.

'Oh OK now I remember. Earlier in the year I went to a movie premier in London. Danny was invited; I was invited on behalf of a fake invitation courtesy of Mr. Storms. We obviously didn't know each other back then so I approached him closer, and introduced myself, and I acted like a real good spy, obviously wired with button cameras, and hearing devices, luckily it was my fourth year so to get a bypass to start early with my first mission was pretty awesome.

Anyway, after I introduced myself, he went on talking to what seemed to look like his body guard, but really Mr. Storms told me it's his boss. The new hi-tech they added to the hearing devices was so good they could actually record it, and it would come out crystal clear. They were talking about Elizabeth and her father especially something about ancient documents . . . The Amber Documents.' Emma gasped.

'The what?' Milan laughed.

'The Amber Documents, It was founded by Amber Storms in eighteen seventy six, like the creator, except her father wrote it. Follow me.' she said and got up, walked towards the front door, down a corridor leading down to a room.

'This is classified, what you see in this room, stays in this room.' she said as she clapped twice. The door closed, and the room went down one level.

'You have an underground level, that's so cool.' Sean smiled.

'Yeah, did you know that Storms Corp. has a one hundred and twenty seventh floor and just keeps on going lower.'

'It's bigger than I remember.' Clayton said

'Well, I had to create a little bit more, for the company.' Emma nodded.

'When did you do it? I was here last year.'

'Well, in the time you weren't here, I added a little more.' she laughed.

'It's colder down here than up there.' Melissa complained.

'I know right.' Emma said and clapped her hands, and the heaters came on. 'There, better?' she said, Melissa nodded. 'Come on, I need to show you something.' she said walking towards an archway which was closed with an armoured door, with a number pad on the right. She turned around to look at Daniel and the others.

'Can you turn around, please . . . you too Clayton.' she ordered with a smile.

Everyone turned around with their backs towards Emma. 'No peaking please.' she said and turned back towards the number pad next to the door, and dialled in her code.

'You can look now.' she finished.

Everyone turned around and followed Emma in the room. They all surround a glass container, which holding eight different coloured diamonds. Four on separate chains and four separate on silver rings.

'They're diamonds? What's the big deal?' Sean asked looking away from the container to Emma.

'Elizabeth's dad ordered these for you guys before you became trainees at the company. I got the designs from him in the beginning of August. The original designs were made in the intelligence bureau in Storms Corporation. Original idea . . . Elizabeth Storms.' she said.

'So this is Elizabeth's idea?' Daniel asked surprisingly.

'I just made it come to life.' she replied.

'What does it do?' Sean asked.

'It transports you to a place . . . say now you're busy with a mission right, and you forgot to retrieve the second item. You can go back to that place and get it if your enemy isn't around, if they're still there well . . .''

'Where are the designs?' Clayton asked.

'They got stolen recently, about a week ago. I'm the Storms Corp. representative. It was in my laptop bag when it was stolen; there was this guy, totally cute. He was telling about his trip to Rome, how exciting. I just got lost for a moment, I wasn't myself. I ended up sleeping on his shoulder, and my laptop was on my lap where it must be, he must have taken it out while I was sleeping.'

'Emma, is this the first time?' Clayton asked.

'No, this was the first time, oh don't you worry it will happen to you too.' she laughed.

'Does Mr. Storms know?' Daniel asked.

'Yes, William was furious.'

'Why?' Milan asked.

'What concern is it of yours?' she snapped.

Milan crossed her arms, and started to wonder around the room.

'Um, Emma can we have ours.' James asked looking down at her hand while pointing to the container.

'In a short while.' she replied calmly.

'Elizabeth wanted a specific colour to go to a certain person then you can pick yours.' she said looking at Daniel.

Emma then walked over to her desk nearby and pulled open a drawer and took out a key, walked back towards the container and opened it. Emma then took out the chain with the royal blue coloured diamond, and placed it around Daniel's neck.

'Unfortunately this diamonds hasn't got its pass from Mr. Storms yet, but hey, I have the authority to give it a pass.' she said and closed the container.

'What about us? We need it too.' James asked. 'I see you already have one.' he finished; pointing down to Emma's finger, where an emerald coloured diamond was on her finger glowing like a glow worm.

'Oh, excuse me.' she said and turned around while she pressed her diamond. The entire room filled with green light, and Emma disappeared with the green light following.

'What the . . .' Sean said in awe.

Moments later Emma appeared in an office at the Storms resident home.

'Emma, I need you to fetch something when things start to get really tough.' Mr. Storms said lying back in his chair. 'I mean this is my daughter I'm talking about and I'm really worried.

'What do you need me to get?' she asked.

'I need you to get the one half of the Amber Documents from the secret underground head-quarters, and the other half from Paulo. If he doesn't want to hand it over, give him a vacation. He could sure use one.' he laughed.

'OK, sir.' Emma replied.

'Please don't call me sir, call me Jeff.' he said looking at her. She pressed her diamond, and disappeared.

'Hey where did she go?' Sean asked. As a green light once again filled the room, Emma had appeared.

'Where did you go?' Daniel asked angrily pushing Emma up against the wall.

'Oh, no wonder Elizabeth likes you, you're very protective. I went to see her father, he gave me new plans. Now please let me go.' Emma laughed, as Daniel let go. 'You know Daniel trust will get you much further.' she finished.

'What are his plans?' Daniel asked.

'That's classified but you will be a part of it, he also assigned Clayton and James to this case. Miguel must stay here with the girls and James's brother' Emma ordered.

'Whoa, wait a sec. I go everywhere with my brother.' Sean cried.

'Well not this time, squirt.' Emma laughed patting him on the shoulder.

'OK, here we go. James you first.' she said as she opened the glass container. James stepped forward and chose a baby blue coloured diamond.'

'I would like the baby blue coloured one.' Milan and the two girls laughed.

'Hey, the diamond calls him.' Emma said seriously.

Milan then kept quiet and rolled her eyes.

'Clayton.' she said and Clayton then stepped forward and chose a clear diamond.

'Mia.' she said. Mia stepped forward.

'Ooh, this one is totally calling me.' she said and chose a ruby coloured diamond ring.

'Melissa.'

'Oh, me right.' she said and stepped forward, and immediately chose a purple ring.

'And last but not least, Milan.' Emma put on a fake smile. Milan smirked and took out a yellow coloured diamond.

'Oh yeah this colour totally calls me. Uh uh.' she said examining the diamond stupidly.

'Come on, where's mine?' Sean asked walking towards the glass container putting his hand inside, Emma then grabbed his arm.

'Sorry, I'm all out, but I'll make you one and send it to you through the mail. OK, that's Elizabeth's and William's 'she said looking at Sean, then back at the container where a pink diamond ring and a black diamond on a chain was placed. She then closed the container.

'We'd better get going.' she replied and walked out the room down a corridor to the next room. Everyone follows her and stands in one line on one side of the room. Emma walks to the other side of the room.

'What's in this room?' Melissa asked

'Well lets see, my laptop, um my paper work and the company's blue prints.' she said pointing everything out and finally walking towards a drawer and opened it. She picked up a gun, to see if it was on safety.

'What's that for?' Milan asked stepping back an inch.

'It is for the bad guys.' Emma laughed, dropping her hand backwards pointing the gun towards the ceiling.

'The company recently sent me new blue prints for a new gadget and I haven't exactly built it yet, but this is what it's gonna look like.' she finished picking up a poster and holding it in front of her, as they all stepped forward.

'It's like some freaky Frankenstein glasses.' Clayton stared at the drawing.

'That's exactly what it is?' she said and dropped her hand. 'It's a special kind of glass, it can only be found in one place in the world.'

'Where will you find it?' Milan asked.

'France.' Emma replied simply.

'Oh, wicked.' James said.

'Hey, what time is it?' Emma asked, looking behind her up to her clock. (It showed 11:30am) She turned around and looked at Daniel, Clayton and James.

'We have to go.' she said.

Placing the blue prints on the desk and walked to them as they moved out of the way. Everyone follows her to the main room where they came from. Emma clapped twice once again and the room started to lift up, to the ground floor.

'Um, the rest of you can make yourselves at home. While you three come with me' she said.

She walked off the platform and out the room, to the living room.

'Wait, you haven't exactly shown us how the diamonds work.' Clayton said, taking her shoulder and turning her around. Emma looked straight into Daniel's eyes and saw grieve.

'Oh, as if we have time for that ... all right, you press the diamond and a holographic screen will appear. Everything, along with options will appear, such as where you want to teleport to. By the way, this doesn't work to teleport to overseas OK, so don't bother. If the company gives the heads up, then I'll insert it. When the diamond blinks your fellow agents are in trouble, then press the diamond softly and you'll teleport automatically to that specific place. The last option, your names have been programmed into the diamond, and you are the only ones in the company that have a special effect on their diamond. Elizabeth and William obviously haven't got theirs, so it will be impossible to get to them.' she explained really fast.

'OK, so tell us how the names work?' Daniel asked, astonished.

'I was getting there, again the holographic screen will come up, there's a list, choose names then your names will appear. Can we go now.' she finished. 'Oh, little tip, you can't touch a holograph, you have to speak to it, whispers work too.' she said and walked to the kitchen.

She walked towards the wall, and took off a car key. She walked back.

'Come on you three.' she said and walked towards the front door and opened it.

'Bye, guys see you later.' James said, and followed her out as Daniel and Clayton followed without a word. Clayton shut the door behind him.

'Can I offer anybody coke?' Miguel asked.

'Yeah, that would be great.' Melissa replied while the others were silent and just fell on the sofa.

Emma opened the garage rolling door with the remote while Daniel, Clayton and James got into the silver Lexus. Emma got into the driver's seat; she placed the gun along with ammunition on the dashboard.

'Are you sure you want that out in the open?' Daniel asked.

'Put it in the compartment then.' she said.

Daniel picked up the gun at the tip. His eyes widen as he opens the compartment and put it in gently, then the ammunition. Emma started to laugh.

'What?'

'That's not the way you handle a gun, don't worry it's on safety.' Emma giggled and closed the compartment for Daniel.

Emma started the car, reversed out into the street. She then drove off the garage doors closed automatically.

'Where are we going?' James asked.

'To Amber.'

'Amber?' Daniel asked.

'The Amber Documents.' Emma replied simply. 'STML much.' she finished, keeping her eyes on the road.

'STML what does that even mean?' Daniel asked

'Short Term Memory Loss, I mentioned it in my living room.' she said, pressing the gas and the car accelerated.

A few minutes later Emma stops the car in front of a little shop. Daniel looks through the windshield.

'Ambers gift shop? Oh, seriously Emma.' Daniel said confused.

'What? It sounds like a person's name, so no one would know. Daniel can you give me that gun?' she asked.

Daniel opened the compartment, and handed it to Emma. He then gave her the ammunition, and closed the compartment. She stopped in a busy street. Emma took out her bag that was in the car and put the gun in there. Emma got out, everyone else followed; she locked the doors, and entered the shop.

This young man approached them.

'Hello, Carlson. How are you man?' Emma greeted him.

'I'm great, did you know it was quiet the whole day.' he replied.

'It's only half of the day that's passed Carl.' Emma laughed.

'Oh, what can I do for you today?' Carlson asked.

'I'd like to see the Amber Documents.' she answered, someone came into the shop.

'I'll be right with you.' he told Emma

'No problem I know where to find it.' she said and turned around and walked to the back of the shop, the three boys followed. She entered through a doorway, and closed it after Daniel, Clayton and James were in the room.

'Where does this room lead?' James asked.

Emma ignored him and clapped twice, the desks went down and hi-tech computers came out.

'Whoa.' Clayton said in awe.

'I wouldn't stand in the middle of the room if I was you cousin.' she said. He moved away and the floor opened and a pedestal came out from the floor with a pad. Emma approached it while the lights dimmed. She dialled in "113B518" suddenly a circle appeared around them, and that piece of floor where they stand moved down along with the pedestal. They stopped softly, on a marble floor, as personnel approached them with detectors. The detector went crazy over Emma's bag.

'It's my gun.' she said quickly, the personnel nodded and they passed them.

They walked up a stairwell and through an open door that lead to long white and grey corridors. Some of the doors where open and as they passed there were agents sitting behind their desks, talking over the phone. An agent stopped them.

'Hey, this is not a place for junior agents.' he said.

'We know, Leo. Move on.' she replied.

He walked off rather fast as if he had to be somewhere.

Emma had finally turned into an office that was empty.

'I just came to fetch something here.' she said as she bended over her desk opened the drawer and took out a card.

'It's the key to the Amber Documents.' she turned around and finished.

'We're going to take it?' James asked.

'No, I'm first going to ask if we can take it. Everyone in this building doesn't know that Elizabeth and William's been kidnapped.' she said looking at all three of them, and then walking out.

They were once again in the long corridors, walking down then turning left; they walked towards a door marked as:

"Director Withard"

Emma then knocks on the door three times and enters. The office is bigger than the rest; it has a living area and golf area but rather small. In the middle stands a desk, with Director Withard (A thin guy with brown eyes and brown hair. He's in a suit.) Who was sitting behind it reading a newspaper.

'Emma, what can I do for you?' the director asks with an American accent.

'Well, it's really a long story.' she said walking towards the director and stopping in front of the desk.

While Daniel, Clayton and James starts to wonder around the office looking around.

'Carry on.' he said.

'OK, well Elizabeth has been kidnapped I don't really know when William was taken. They're willing to exchange them for the Amber Documents . . ."

'You know we separated them, Emma.'

'Yeah, Mr. Storms said I have to get it.'

'And you know they're just copies.'

'No they're not, we have to get the copies and give Mr. Storms the original ones, so you haven't been sitting here for nothing.' she said knowingly.

'Did you know the copies are empty?'

'Yes, but they won't open it until we're gone. Did I pass the test? Can I have the documents now, this is serious.' she said hesitating moving forward, putting her hands on the desk.

'Alright I'll give you permission, but only if I can supervise you.' he said looking at the three boys, who were now standing behind her. He then stood up, walked around his desk passes them heading towards the door.

'Come then.' he finished.

He left the door open for them and walked down the corridor to the other end of the passage, the four of them following him.

They stopped in front of the door.

'Emma did you bring your key.'

'Yes, I have it sir.' she said handing him her key.

He swiped it through the device and the door opened automatically. All five of them entered, the door closed behind them. The room was white like the entrance hall.

'Guys, this is Amber.' Emma said. They all surrounded a glass stand with the document wrapped in leather.

The papers were old and coffee coloured, the leather was torn on one side.

The director walked over to a table took off an armoured case. He walked back.

'Put it in here.' he said putting the case on a table next to the documents. 'Be careful. It's very frail' he said as he help Emma place it in the case.

'Thank you, sir.' she said and closed the case.

'How are you going to get there?' the director asked.

'With a new gadget the company developed this week.' Emma replied.

'Oh, yeah, just remember that the documents have been split.'

'Yeah I'm pretty sure, Mr. Storms has the fatal part of it which will destroy the company.' she said and handed the case to Withard.

'Where are you going?' James asked.

'I'm going to fetch the other piece. I'll be right back, OK.' she replied. She took a few steps away from them and pressed her diamond, and her list of options appeared. She said names, then a list of names. She announces Paulo, and suddenly an emerald colour filled the room and Emma disappeared along with the green light.

A house, in a quiet street is disturbed by an emerald light in the kitchen window.

'Paulo are you here?' Emma shouted leaving the kitchen into the living room where Paulo sat in a chair.

'What?' he asked simply.

'I need the other half of the documents; its urgent Elizabeth and William have been kidnapped. The nappers want the documents.' Emma said urgently.

'No, the documents hold confidential information and I have protected it all this time. I'm not just gonna let it go.' he said. He got up and stood almost right up against Emma

'OK, you're obviously upset about Elizabeth and William's capture.' she said as she took one step back. 'But they're more important than the documents, besides we're gonna fetch the duplicate at the company . . . how would you like to finally go on vacation?' she changed the topic.

'Wow that sounds great, who would I go with?' he asked Emma.

'Um, you might meet someone there, where ever you are going. Maybe even your true love. And if you want that to happen you have to give me the documents.' she said hoping he would fall for it.

'All right Emma, you always know where to push a button.' he said with a smile and hugged her. 'Come on I'll show you where it is.'

'This guy is seriously demented.' Emma thought to herself, and then followed him.

'This is where I put it.' he said pointing down to his pillow case.

'It is in the pillow case?' Emma asked.

'What? It's the simplest place, burglars won't look in the simplest place they'd rather blow up a safe.' he laughed, and Emma smiled.

Paulo then picked up his pillow and dug in it and took out the documents, and slowly handed it over to her. 'Please take care of her.' he said.

'Don't worry Paulo she is in safe hands.' Emma replied.

'Can I offer you a drink, cool drink?' Paulo asked.

'No thanks, I'm kind of in a hurry. Hey but thanks anyway.' she said and pressed her diamond, Emma once again disappeared with the same green light.


The green light filled the strong room where the other half of the Amber Documents was held. But no one was waiting for her. She walked towards the door and opened it.

'Emma?' she heard from behind. She turned around really fast. 'Did you get it?'

'Yeah, I got it.' she said holding up the documents in her hand. 'Err, Director Withard we might have to give Paulo a long holiday.' she said while the three boys walked towards her.

'I'll work on it.' he said and gave Emma the armoured suitcase. He then turned around walked back to his office. 'See you around Emma.'

'Come on let's go.' she said and walked in the opposite direction.

'Um isn't the exit the other way.' James asked pointing his hand next to his face while walking forward.

'No, that was the entrance, this way is the exit.' she said not turning around to face them.

They were already outside getting in the car when Carlson came running out.

'EMMA? Wait Mr. Storms says he's got something to tell you. He's on the phone.' he said entering his shop again.

'Guys get in, I'm coming.' she said and walked towards the shop door and entered. Emma walked towards the phone and picked it up.

'Hello.' Emma said surprisingly.

'Emma, don't bring the documents we have a problem here at Storms Corp. keep it with you . . .' he said. Emma heard his office door open. 'Um, OK. Bring me the blue prints first then I'll decide.' he finished and he hung up the phone.

Emma turned around and ran out the door jumped into the car, started it, and drove off.

'What's the problem?'

'Elizabeth's father encountered trouble at the company, we can't take it there. He said I have to keep it with me.' she said rushing off down the road and back to her house.

# CHAPTER 10

# THE AMBER DOCUMENTS

Emma stopped the Lexus next to her red pick-up. Unlocked all the doors, and got out. Daniel, Clayton and James followed her lead. Clayton looked at Emma and took out the armoured case. Emma walked around the car swinging the bag around onto her back, and stopped next to Clayton.

'We should hurry. I have to make another phone call, could you take this and that in for me.' she said handing her bag to Daniel and pointing to the armoured case. 'I'll be right in' she finished looking up teary eyed.

'OK, come on guys.' Clayton ordered.

'Hey, Daniel we'll get Elizabeth, don't worry.' she said assuringly as Daniel nodded and turned around and carried on walking with Clayton and James.

Emma waited for them to get into the house, and then she took her phone out of her pocket. Emma quickly dialled the number of the kidnappers; she put the cell phone to her ear.

## A FEW MOMENTS LATER

'Hello Emma.' the man said rudely.

'Can I speak to William?' Emma asked discourteously.

'Sorry he's a bit tied up.' he snorted.

'You listen to me, I speak to him or you don't get the . . .' Emma was interrupted.

'I'll kill him . . . don't listen to him Emma.' Emma could hear William's voice, she covered her mouth. She got shivers up her spine.

'NO, PLEASE. Let me talk to him.' Emma cried.

'Listen, here doll face. I'll tell you where the rendezvous point is, OK. It's in a warehouse between Van Reenen and Ladysmith. You give us the documents. And we give you Elizabeth, and your boyfriend. The dead line is seventeen hundred hours and if all fails, I'll kill both of them.' he said and hung up.

Emma looked up to the sky, and a tear started to fall. Emma walked over to the wall separating her from the neighbours, and slide down slowly to the ground. She looked out to the street, she saw some kids walked past laughing and making jokes. The neighbours across the street took their dogs for a walk and had just returned. Tears started to fill her eyes again and she looked up to the blue sky once again.

'Hi, Emma.' she heard from above, the next door neighbour's ten year old daughter Melanie appeared. She was blond with brown eyes.

Emma looked away quickly and wiped away her tears.

'Hey, Melanie.' she said sadly, looking up.

'Are you OK, Emma?' Melanie asked with a frown

Emma then got up, turned around to face Melanie.

'Yeah, every thing's fine. Just had an emotional break down, it happens to everyone.' Emma explained.

'Oh, OK see you around Emma.' she said and disappeared behind the other side of the wall.

Emma turned away and walked straight towards the small red gate that Daniel, Clayton and James had used. She walked to the front door, opened it and went in. Everyone was sitting in the living room quietly, waiting for Emma.

'He gave us a dead line.' Emma said walking into the living room.

'When is it?' Daniel asked curiously.

'Five O'clock tonight.' she replied distinctively. Daniel stood up.

'Why?' he asked.

'They don't know that we already have the documents.' she said and her cell phone rang. 'Hello?' Emma asked.

'Emma, change of plans. The problem has seemed to resolve itself. You can bring the documents.' Jeff said without greeting her.

'That's great news. Speaking of news, I'll tell you when I bring it.' she smiled.

'OK, do what you need to do, to get here.' he replied and then hung up.

Emma put her phone away and looked slowly at everybody in the room.

'I need the documents, Mr. Storms wants it. That means Daniel, you must come with me.' she said.

She and Daniel's diamonds started to blink.

'Remember what I told you?' she asked as Daniel nodded. Emma then pressed her diamond softly, and disappeared with an emerald light filling the room.

Daniel looked over at everybody, everyone started to speak at once.

'Go, Daniel.' they said together as he looked down at his diamond and pressed it.

Daniel felt himself being pulled by the stomach, all he could see was a royal blue light tunnel. Suddenly he found himself in Elizabeth's father's office. Emma was already speaking to Jeff, when Daniel came. He was holding the armoured suit case.

Elizabeth's father called him. Daniel walked over to them and placed the case on the desk. Jeff opened the case and in the middle was the Amber Documents. He took it out slowly and put it in a different case. One of Jeff's agents stepped forward, and handed Jeff the fake documents. The leather was torn on one side and the pages were aged like the real ones.

'Emma, I want you to keep the other piece. Keep it close to your heart, and no one will take it. This is the full empty paged document that looks surreal.' Jeff said wisely.

'Yes, Jeff.' she nodded.

'What was the news?' Jeff asked.

'The kidnappers gave us a deadline. Five pm. It's in a warehouse between Van Reenen and Ladysmith' she answered.

'Five pm, means they don't know if you have the documents yet, and it's not so far away from where you are. Listen you need to go, give it to them early. So that they don't think you're pulling something. Daniel, you and your friends said you want to handle this alone. But it has come to an end. Let's get this over with.' he said seriously. Getting up, handing the suitcase to Daniel and leaving his office.

'Now what are we going to do?' Daniel asked Emma looking over at the man who was still standing in Elizabeth's father's office.

'We go back.' she said simply taking a few steps back. 'See you around Cory.' she smiled and pressed her diamond and said 'Home.' and she disappeared with the green light filing the room.

Daniel pressed his diamond.

'Um, Emma's house.' he said and he could feel once again, the pulling feeling, and the blue light. He found himself holding the armoured suitcase in Emma's living room. Everyone's clapping and shouting.

'Well done Dan.' Milan shouted. 'How does it feel to teleport?'

'Fantastic.' he replied as everyone cheered.

'HEY!, there's no time to celebrate. The only time we can celebrate is when Elizabeth and William are in safe hands.' Emma said seriously.

Everyone stopped cheering, and silence had filled the room. 'We need to get going.' she announced.

Everyone scrambled to get their stuff together and they all ran out the door. Emma took a different set of keys, and the Lexus's keys, and locked the front door. Once outside Emma ran to the garage open the door and pulled the Lexus into the garage. She came out of the garage and rolled down the door again.

'I'll be right back.' Emma said and disappeared to the back of the house.

A few minutes later, Emma's driving a white van from the back of the house. She stops in the driveway and everyone gets in.

## RENDEZVOUS UNIT

Emma stopped the van; everyone looks out to the left. It's cloudy and only a little sunlight was shinning through.

Is that it, there?' Milan asked pointing out into an open field.

'Yep, it's the only warehouse between Van Reenen and Ladysmith.' Emma said with an irritation to her voice. 'Do you see Elizabeth's father anywhere?'

'No.' Daniel replied.

'OK, let's get down to business.' she said and turned the van onto the gravel road leading to the warehouse. 'Does anybody know what time it is?' she asked as everyone looked down at their watches. Daniel was the only one to answer.

'It's half-past three.'

Emma stopped the van just a few meters away from the warehouse entrance; they could see the entrance was big enough for a car to fit through. The warehouse was all rusted and old, with white plastics covering the windows

'This is where they must have gone in.' Milan said knowingly.

'No, hey what do you think?' Emma said rudely.

'Don't be so rude, I'm just trying to help. Milan cried.

We're all trying to help. We all want Elizabeth back.' Daniel said putting his hand on her shoulder. 'So, are we in this together?' Daniel said looking at everyone.

'You're right; don't know why I'm so worked up. Sorry, Milan you're smart and you just point out the obvious.' Emma said looking at Milan with a smile.

'It's OK I could see you we're troubled from the beginning.' she replied, smiling back at Emma.

'Are you ready for this? This is your first mission and it won't be easy.'

'Yeah!' they all said together.

'Daniel could you take out the documents?' she asked.

'Yes.' he replied and got out taking the armoured case with him.

Emma was the next to get out and everyone else got out one at a time.

'Which one of you can drive?' she asked as Milan's hand shot up. 'I should have known. I need you to pull out into the field.' she said giving the keys to Milan when she came and fetched it.

Milan ran back to the van, started it and drove off into the field.

'Sean, James and Melissa, you'll be the stealthy ones. Only if things start to go really bad can you make some noise.' she said as Milan was already heading back. 'Daniel and Clayton you'll be my wing-men. Milan, Mia and Miguel, you'll be the stay behinds.' she ordered.

Emma turned around and walked towards the entrance, Daniel and Clayton followed along with Sean, James and Melissa. They were all standing in the entranceway. From the outside everything looked dark, but once they were in, they saw the two SUV's parked very skew from each other inside. The walls of the warehouse were black from soot of a fire that was there before.

'I hope I don't pee in my pants.' Sean whispered as everyone looked over at him.

Milan laughed softly at a joke Miguel was telling her.

'Anyway, you three come with me.' she said as they followed her to one side of the warehouse.

'OK, be as quiet as you possibly can. If you see pieces of metal don't step on it. If you see a rat, don't scream rather pee in your pants.' she said as Melissa snorted, then trying to hold her laugh. 'OK you can go now.' she ordered pointing the way out for them.

Melissa, Sean and James tip-toed silently towards the iron steps and started to go up one level.

Emma walked back to the others; she slowly slid her bag down her arm to her hand. She zipped it open and took out a small explosive and placed it underneath the first car next to the wheel.

'What are you doing?' Daniel whispered rolling his eyes to Clayton and he just lifted his shoulders and raised his eyebrows.

'It's a timer, I set it to go off in thirty minutes.' she whispered. She got out from underneath the car. Daniel and Clayton helped her up.

'This is the two SUV's that chased us around town.' Daniel told Emma.

'Thanks. Really' she said and walked over to the next car.

'Yeah.' a few seconds later Emma pulled herself out from under the second car.

'Uh, which way do we go?' James asked, they were standing in front of a door and a corridor that leads somewhere.

'I think we should take the room.' Clayton suggested.

'Uh uh, that way is too obvious. We have to take the corridor.' Emma said, pointing towards it.

Daniel and Clayton followed her down the corridor. The long thin corridor makes a left turn, and leads down to another room. They pass some small rooms, some of them with doors and some of them without doors. One door at the end of the corridor, had a light shining from underneath it, and shadows passing underneath and they could hear voices on the other side of the door. Emma walked straight towards the door and knocked on it with confidence. A few minutes later the door opened, and a guy holding a gun in his left hand standing in the doorway.

'Ah, Emma, great to see you here.' he said slowly dropping the gun to the ground. 'And you brought company.'

'Yeah, they are. And they're Elizabeth's friends.' she replied.

They hesitated to walk into the room but walked in anyway.

Daniel was the only one to look up and see Sean, James and Melissa's shadows on the wall behind them on the second level.

There were four men in the room, two on each side of the door, one with William and Elizabeth who were conscious, but they were tied up and their mouths duck taped. They were looking at Emma, without a word.

Emma turned around and nodded at Daniel; he walked around her and slammed the case on a nearby table.

A door on the far left opened and a man came in.

'Danny?' Emma said surprised

Elizabeth started to cry and everyone looked over at her. The man who was watching Elizabeth and William hit her in the face.

'Hey!' Daniel shouted running towards her and kicking the man hard on his leg. The man turned around and hit Daniel also in the face. Danny laughed rudely.

'Thanks for the delivery.' he laughed. 'And a bit early too, you're desperate.' he said in an irritating English accent.

'Let Daniel go.' Emma said angrily.

The man was holding Daniel down. Danny nodded and the man let Daniel go by pushing him towards the ground.

Danny opened the case, and slowly lifted the fake documents opened the seal and slowly paged through it. He looked up at Emma who was now wide-eyed staring at Daniel, who starting sitting up.

'Thank you.' Danny said, aiming the gun straight at Emma's chest.

'NO!' Clayton shouted. William also shouted with the duck tape around his mouth. It was too late, Danny had already pulled the trigger and Emma fell to the ground. Clayton was frozen with fear. Daniel jump up and ran to Clayton.

Danny turned to Daniel pointing the gun at him. Daniel stopped in his tracks.

'Hold up, do you honestly think I would fall for this?' Danny asked waving the fake documents around roughly. Loose papers flew out of the leather case.

'Is this a set up?' he asked, walking towards Daniel.

'No.' Daniel shook his head quickly.

'Well, it looks like one to me. You see this is what happens when you try to play an enemy. Where are the originals?' he asked throwing the documents in Daniel's face.

'I don't know.' Daniel said nervously, looking over at Emma and Clayton, who was now kneeling next to Emma. Daniel saw him lean forward and Emma's lips moving.

The next moment Daniel heard a second gun go off and when he looked back at Danny, he saw him falling towards the ground. Daniel then grabbed the gun from Danny. Sean, James and Melissa jumped down from the top floor to this level.

Daniel turned around and pointed the gun at the man who was watching Elizabeth and William.

'Move aside slick.' he said.

'Hey, didn't you hear him. He said move aside.' Clayton said now standing next to Daniel.

'I got a black belt, and I'm not afraid to use it.' Melissa said nervously, as one of the men standing at the door stepped towards her. Without knowing it, she did a high kick and the man fell to the ground.

James then stepped forward and boxed the second man in the stomach while Melissa kicked him in the face when he bent down.

'Hey, that's pretty good.' he said looking over at her.

'You're out numbered.' Clayton sang.

The man then moved three steps away.

Daniel ran towards Emma and William. Clayton aims the gun on the last man. Daniel first cut the ropes on William and he shot up running straight to Emma.

'Emma?' he asked.

'I'll be OK, it's just shock.' she replied with a smile, taking out the real document from her jacket, with a bullet still sitting there in the leather cover. William started to laugh. 'William I put explosions on their cars to go off within thirty minutes, and I think there's only two minutes left.' William's smile vanished, and he pulled Emma up quickly.

'Hey, we have to get out of here.' William said looking over at Elizabeth who was now free.

William, supporting Emma ran out the door, as everyone else follows. It was a race towards the door but everyone got out safely, just in time, before the explosions went off.

Milan, Mia and Miguel watched in shock, as everyone dived for cover. When everything settled down, everyone got up from the ground, and started to cheer.

'Oh, I am definitely gonna feel that in the morning.' Emma said holding her chest. 'Honestly it feels like someone punched me there. If it wasn't for your father, I wouldn't be here.' she told William and Elizabeth who were standing with her.

'Oh, so is that what it meant. "Keep it near your heart and no one will take it".' Daniel smiled wrapping his arms around her. Emma smiled.

'Well at least we're all safe.' Emma smiled as she looked up and saw a SC chopper came in to land a few meters from them, and the first Police van appeared behind the trees beside the road.

'Dad . . . dad.' Elizabeth yelled and as soon as the chopper landed she ran towards her father.

Mr. Storms opened the door and ran towards his daughter and hugging her.

'Mom?' she cried. Walking over to her and hugging her.

'You know, I thought for a second I was gonna loose you.' William told Emma waving at his father, while putting his arm around her and walking towards the chopper.

'Elizabeth!' Milan and Mia shouted together running up to her and doing some sort of dance routine when Melissa joined them.

The sun had finally come out behind the clouds, just in time to set with a golden shine in the west.

William turned to Emma and looked her deep in the eyes as they closed in on each other and they kissed.

Daniel looked over at Elizabeth as she looked back with a laugh. William looked over at Elizabeth and smiled

'Well, done agents.' Jeff said proudly.

'Dad, did you know Melissa has a black belt in karate?'

'Yeah, that's my little secret.' Melissa laughed.

'Really, wow. Sean would you like to join the company when you're older?' Jeff asked him.

'Not really. This is not my world I'll leave it to my brother.' Sean smiled.

'Anybody want a ride?' Mr. Storms asked.

Milan, Mia, Melissa and Elizabeth's hands shot up, followed by Daniel, Clayton, James, Miguel and Sean.

'I'll ride with Emma, dad.' William told his father.

'OK.' he replied and waved them goodbye. Everyone got in the SC chopper one by one. Emma and William waved back, as the rotary blades started, they lifted and flew off.

The police men came out of the warehouse with Danny and the others handcuffed, pushing them into one of the vans to take them to the police station.

William turned towards Emma and hugged her again as they watched the chopper, fly off.

# A WEEK LATER

Elizabeth's house was slamming with noise; it was a celebration, for the documents were safe at Storms Corp. for ever.

'A toast! To the Amber Documents, and to Emma. To Elizabeth's friends. Congratulations you have been moved on early to full time training, for your effort and team work.' Jeff said with a smile.

Emma's phone rang.

'Hello?' she answered.

'Hello, is this Emma?' a man said with an Australian accent

'Yes this is her speaking.' she replied closing her one ear and standing up and walking away from the noise. Emma walked around the corner; there was a big garden with two tennis courts.

'Sound like a fun party.'

'Who is this?' she asked.

'Don't you recognize my voice.' the man said with a surprising ring to his voice.

'Uncle Stephens?' she smiled.

William peered around the corner and walking towards her when she turned around and saw him.

'Hello.' Uncle Stephens replied.

'It's been a long time uh.' she laughed looking up at William, with shiny eyes.

'Yeah, I'm coming to visit in December. I already told your father about it he said its fine. Is it OK with you?' her uncle asked unsure.

'Yeah, that's great. Of course.' she replied.

'OK, bye bye.'

'Bye, Uncle Stephens.' she replied and hung up.

'Uncle Stephens is coming to visit?' he asked and she nodded.

William looked at her and walked up to her.

'Come on, we're missing a party.' he smiled, and escorted her back.

Everybody was dancing to the music and having fun; someone got off balance and fell over laughing.

Anna is walking towards them.

'Emma, how are you doing? Long time no see, hey?'

'Yes, nice to see you too Anna.' she said hugging her.

'Huh, William can I talk to you for a sec?' Anna turned to William.

'Emma, I'll be right back.' William said and gave Emma a little squeeze on her arm

'OK.' she smiled and Anna and William walked away.

'William, she's a beauty have you popped the Q yet?' Anna asked with a wide smile. William looked over at her. Elizabeth pulled Emma aside to go dance with them.

'No, but I am thinking about it.' he whispered.

'You'd better hurry, cause the company hottest are getting a piece of her, and you know what I just realized?'

'What?' William asked with curiosity.

'I need the loo. See you later' she said and turned around and walked towards the front door.

William laughed. He then ran towards Emma and joined her and the others on the dance floor.

## THAT NIGHT

Elizabeth was sitting in her room doing her weekend homework, when her cell phone rang.

'Hello?'

'Look by your phone, do you see it?' a man said.

'Who's this?' she asked. Before she could ask again the man hung up the phone.

Elizabeth then got up and walked over to her phone and found a mini camera charm with a note underneath it. Elizabeth picked up the note and it read: "Your every move is being watched and your conversations recorded. Tell this to anyone and force will be put out onto them. With compliments from Gemini Industries." she looked up and ran towards her window and peered out looking for anybody who might be watching her. She shut the window and drew the curtains closed.

## TWO DAYS LATER AT EMMA'S HOUSE

It was early morning when Emma woke up from a loud bang, and distinct voices.

'Find her.' a man said with a Russian accent.

She got out of bed wearing boy shorts and a spaghetti top, and ran to her door and peered out. She saw three men in black clothes.

'Dirt, this is damn dirt.' She whispered loudly turning around and running silently to her cupboard, taking out her gun and loading it. She walked out the door.

'HEY!' she said as the Russian man turned his head.

'You're trespassing.' she said walking slowly towards him.

The two men in black were now behind her, when she turned around she did a turn kick and kicked them in the face and then tripping them by doing a low kick.

'Uh, nice try but I'm afraid you're still out numbered.' he said pointing at the door, Emma still approaches him and the gun still aiming at him. She looked out the door at about six men where standing in her yard with guns.

'Miss Emma, you need to come with us.'

'There is no way . . . Gemini Industries that's a stupid name.' she said reading from his jacket.

'Move.' she said now aiming the gun at his head.

'William what is this?' she said after the simulator shut off.

She dropped her hand with the gun, and she was in the Storms Corp. simulator room, looking up at William.

'Who's 'Gemini Industries?' she asked

'It is our newest enemy.' William replied simply.

'Great, another enemy.' she sighed, placing the gun on a nearby altar and heading for the steps leading up to the control room.

'Are you kidding me?' she said as she closed the door behind her.

'Nope, this is for real. Well not the simulations. We even got a real Russian to do the voice over.' he laughed.

'This isn't funny.' she smiled. 'Come on let's go.'

'Err, don't you want to change.' he laughed again.

'Don't you mean put my clothes on?'

A few moments later they left the control room and headed for the elevator.

'Do you want coffee?'

'Yeah, that'd be great.' she smiled. The elevator doors close.

# About the Author

I did homeschooling up to Grade 10 in 2005. I start writing my first novel after that and finished in May 2009 but never get to publish it, continuously editing and changing the manuscript where I think it will improve the story line.

I am working in a book & stationery shop during the day and in quiet times think of plots that can being developed in a possible story. I received a book award from the local library for a short story competition that I entered in 2007. I also wrote a few short stories that is still unpublished but kept in a safe place for later use.

I love horse riding and have my own horse kept on a nearby farm of a friend and go as many times as possible for a day. I grew up in Cape Town but moved to Harrismith in the Freestate South Africa when I was 11 years and still lives here.